AN ILLINOIS CHRISTMAS ANTHOLOGY

an *Illinois*

Christmas

anthology

Edited by

Stephen E. Engels
Theresa Rice Engels

Partridge Press
St. Cloud, Minnesota

Editors: Theresa R. Engels and Stephen E. Engels
Original Art: Ethel Boyle
Typography: North Star Press of St. Cloud, Inc.
Cover Design: Ann Blattner
Post Card Art from the collections of Elizabeth Engels and Miranda Briggs
About the Cover: "Ice Skating in Krape Park" by Merl Blackwood,
part of the permanent collection of the Freeport Art
Museum.

The vivid painting by Merl Blackwood attests to a long tradition of skating and Christmas activities in Freeport, Illinois, as a rival city's newspaper reported much earlier:

Metropolitan Airs

Freeport is putting on metropolitan airs. A skating park has recently been instituted there at a heavy expense, which will be opened with a grand display on Christmas Day. It is the intention to have the band present every evening during the skating season to add zest to the enjoyment.

Galena Weekly Gazette, December 26, 1865

ISBN: 0-9621085-2-9
Copyright © 1991

Partridge Press
P. O. Box 364
St. Cloud, Minnesota, 56302
612-253-1145

For Christmas, with its lots an' lots of candies, cakes an' toys,
Was made, they say, for proper kids an' not for naughty boys;
So wash yer face an' bresh yer hair, an' mind yer p's and q's,
An' don't bust out yer pantaloons, an' don't wear out yer shoes;
Say "Yessum" to the ladies, an' "Yessur" to the men,
An' when they's company, don't pass yer plate for pie again;
But, thinking of the things yer'd like to see upon that tree,
Jest 'fore Christmas be as good as yer kin be!

Eugene Field
Jest 'Fore Christmas

CONTENTS

KEEPING CHRISTMAS

FROM MAIN STREET TO STATE STREET

CELEBRATING THE FEAST

CELEBRATING THE NATIVITY

CHRISTMAS RECIPES

STORIES AND POEMS TO READ ALOUD

Newspaper accounts of Christmas in Illinois: The *Rockford Journal, Ottawa Free Trader, Chicago Tribune, Galena Weekly Gazette, Bloomington Daily Pantagraph, Chicago Sun-Times, Ottawa Republican, Champaign County Gazette.*

Keeping Christmas

Christmas, dear delightful Christmas, with it's crowd of youthful recollections and joyous associations, is again with us bringing to the "young'uns" high expectations of visits from that saintly goblin of youthful fancy, old Santa Claus, who, generous-hearted, jolly old hombre, comes stealthily, with well stocked pack and furred feet, to fill the stocking duly suspended by chimney corner, with brightly painted toys and gaily decorated sweet-meats. The Christian feels his faith strengthened and his hope brightened at the return of this sacred festival. To each and all we most kindly wish a "Merry Christmas."

Ottawa Free Trader, December 14, 1847

Turkey, Plum Pudding and Mince Pie

My whole family, I think, enjoy since we have been here much better health than in England, and we have enjoyed the fine Indian summer, which has lasted full two months, of most charming temperature, the thermometer varying from 70 to 75. We had only two wet days in November, and one sudden change to 35 degrees; the weather in December was equally fine till Christmas-day, when we had frost and snow much as in England, and since that time some very cold days, the thermometer being below freezing, 22 degrees. We have now milder weather, but frost and snow on the ground, and the thermometer again at freezing, but gently thawing.

On Christmas day, we invited our party as at Marden, my late residence in Hertfordshire: we assembled thirty-two in number.

A more intelligent, sensible collection I never had under my roof in my own country. A plentiful supply of plum pudding, roast beef and mince pies were at table, and turkeys in plenty, having purchased four for a dollar the preceding week. We found among the party good musicians, good singers; the young people danced nine couple, and the whole party were innocently cheerful and happy during the evening. The company were pleased to say I had transferred Old England and its comforts to the Illinois. Thus, my dear Sir, we are not in want of society; and I would not change my situation for any in America, nor for *disturbed* or *tumultuous* England.

Richard Flower, 1820

The First Christmas Tree

by Gustave Koerner

A day or two before Christmas I went, on terribly bad roads and in a disagreeable drizzle of half snow and half rain, to St. Louis to buy a present for Sophie, and for myself, Blackstone's Commentaries on the English Law, a classic book, for which I paid five dollars.

On my return from St. Louis on the evening of the twenty-fourth, I passed through Belleville after dark. In spite of the mud in the streets they were very lively. The Americans celebrate Christmas in their own way. Young and old fired muskets, pistols

and Chinese fire-crackers, which, with a very liberal consumption of egg-nog and tom-and-jerry, was the usual, and in fact, the only mode of hailing the arrival of the Christ-Child (Christ-Kindchen).

On Christmas day, 1833, we had a Christmas tree, of course. In our immediate neighborhood we had no evergreen trees or bushes. But Mr. Engelmann had taken the top of a young sassafras tree, which still had some leaves on it, had fixed it into a kind of pedestal, and the girls had dressed the tree with ribbons and bits of colored paper and the like, had put wax candles on the branches, and had hung it with little red apples and nuts and all sorts of confectionery, in the making of which Aunt Caroline was most proficient. Perhaps this was the first Christmas tree that was ever lighted on the banks of the Mississippi.

Early Chicago Customs
by Fernando Jones

I can tell you all about every Christmas with the exception of one or two since 1835. That's a long time, isn't it? Still it seems but a little while ago. There were no fountain pens nor hacks with rubber wheels then. Nor Christmas trees. I don't remember when it was I saw my first one. They are a new contraption; but pretty. I like to see the tinsel and the filigree work, the toy tops that act almost human and children around them singing to the music of some band or other. But shucks! They are as straw and saw dust compared to the old fashioned trees.

I remember the first Catholic Church and the first services, conducted in it, at Christmas. The priest was a learned, righteous man, and he preached earnestly. The church was located over on Lake Street—a little bit of a wooden thing not much bigger than a box car.

It was quickly filled and for 100 feet around on each side of the little place, men and women gathered and stood in the snow and cold until the benediction was pronounced.

We had 1,000 people when I took the first census of the village a year after I landed. No one was in debt, malice and mischief were unknown. Health was good; sickness unheard of. There were no champagne orgies, no midnight balls, no lobster salad or mince pies to battle with. Our worst enemy was an occasional pack of wolves.

Before another issue of our paper Merry Christmas will have dawned upon our homes. The season brought its peculiar attractions to lend a charm to the occasion, a charm at least to those for whom there are no terrors in sharp biting cold, clear glittering ice for the skaters steel, and well trod snowy paths for the flying sleighs. To all who have bright home fires, high heaped with fuel, and plenty in basket and in store, this Monarch of the Holidays is all the merrier in a crystal setting, garbed in the full court attire of King Winter.

Chicago Tribune, December 24, 1859

Metropolitan Airs

Freeport is putting on metropolitan airs. A skating park has recently been instituted there at a heavy expense, which will be opened with a grand display on Christmas Day. It is the intention to have the band present every evening during the skating season to add zest to the enjoyment.

Galena Weekly Gazette, December 26, 1865

On Monday, which day was generally observed here as Christmas, there were numerous young men and ladies on the ice of Galena River, enjoying the health-giving sport of skating. The mercury was nearly down to zero, and the wind freezing cold, but little did the skaters heed it. On they dashed, full of glee, bidding defiance to the North wind, and enjoying the fun with a hearty zest. Numbers of spectators gathered on the bridge and the river banks to witness the sport. There were several fine skaters in the party, among the most graceful of whom were some half a dozen Misses from ten to fifteen years of age.

Galena Weekly Gazette, January 3, 1871

December

Hoary, frosty, drear December!
Bleakest of the winter months!
Very well do I remember
How I loved to greet thee once.
In my boyhood's happy hours—
In my days of youthful prime—
Then I loved thy sweeping tempests,
Then I loved the wintertime. . . .

Now that I am growing older,
And the frosts of years appear,
The current of my blood runs colder—
Thy snows becoming still more drear.
Let me escape thy chilling presence,
Dreariest of the dreary months!
I cannot greet thee as of yore,
Or love thee as I loved thee once.

Thomas Gregg, 1847

With Grant's Army in Virginia
by Charles A. Humphreys

Friday, December 23, reveille sounded at five again, and with a breakfast of coffee alone, we started. Our rations and forage were now exhausted, and for the rest of our journey we must live on the country. In the course of the day our headquarters forager brought in two hams, a spare-rib, and enough flour for several days. We marched until eleven o'clock that night, and encamped under the cold light of stars on a side hill so steep that we had to crawl on our hands and knees to keep from falling. The top of the snow was frozen into a hard crust which the horses' hoofs scarcely broke. However, we made ourselves comfortable with a log fire, a supper of coffee, ham, and griddle cakes, and a bed of boughs, and after five hours we started again.

Our regimental position this day was in the rear of the column, a very uncomfortable place to be in when the column is long and the roads are bad. There were many places where an obstruction or break in the road made it impossible for more than two horses to pass abreast; and as we generally marched by fours, the column at such places would be drawn out to twice its normal length; and if the advance moved steadily it would get away eight or ten miles from the rear at such an obstruction, and then the rear companies, after having waited to let the others pass the obstacle, would have to gallop to close up the column. Generally, however, at such a place, the advance waits for the rear to catch up, as a caterpillar when it meets an obstruction huddles up, fixes its tail, then lengthens out over the obstacle, fixes its head and, drawing in its lengthened body, huddles up again and then creeps on as before with equal length. Besides this unevenness of motion, a position in the rear is also unpleasant from the sights one has to witness. On this day we passed hundreds of horses worn out by the toilsome march and left dead by the side of the road; and we kept passing dismounted men who could not keep up with the column, some of them with boots worn through and a few barefoot and leaving tracks of blood in the frozen crust. That night we got into camp at nine o'clock, cold, tired, and hungry; still we brightened up a little to think it was Christmas Eve, and that our friends at home were enjoying it in quiet comfort and happy meetings, even though we could not enjoy it, but must spread our cold and cheerless tables in the presence of those enemies who otherwise would make our home firesides cold and cheerless as our own.

Next day was Sunday, December 25th, and as we woke, the "Merry Christmas" wishes went around, but always with the added wish for a merrier Christmas next year.

We forded this day the two branches of the Rappahannock, having first to cut a passage through the ice that covered the river. In our march we often had to dismount and lead our horses down the steep hills, sliding with them most of the way. Their shoes were now so smooth that they with difficulty kept from falling even on level ground. Our sufferings this day from the cold were very severe. Our feet were almost frozen, encased as they were in wet and frozen boots, and dangling in the frosty air. There is not sufficient exercise in the slow motion of a cavalry column to send the warm blood away down to the feet. Our only relief was a partial one when the column halted—in stamping upon the ground.

On the Tented Field

A Merry Christmas to you all, good readers! Today heralds the advent of another Christmas to be celebrated by our people. On this honored morn many joyous reunions take place; loving hearts again will hold sweet intercommunication. Little folks will joyously bless Kris Kringle for his benevolent fore-thought in making them so many presents, and have all the more faith in the innocent traditions of childhood. There will be some heavy hearts too, hearts that one year ago partook of Christmas cheer with some loved one, now passed beyond the ken of mortals perchance upon the field of battle. A sad Christmas it is for such! May the one whose advent the day commemorates heal their wounded hearts. Let us also remember that while we hold Christmas merrymaking that there are thousands of gallant hearts who also have Christmas memories. But on the tented field, far from home they will have no Christmas such as in times past was wont to make their hearts joyous. Yet many a soldier while treading his lonely beat with nothing but the blue sky above and cold earth beneath, worn and battlestained, will feel his heart warm within him as on Christmas Eve he thinks of the loved circle at home, and a silent prayer for their welfare will ascend to the God of the Sabbath from the lips of the soldier of Freedom. Good people remember those soldiers today. We give you today our Christmas greeting with the hope that ere another year passes our greeting can be mingled the benison of "Peace on earth and good will to men."

Bloomington Daily Pantagraph, December 25, 1862

To Fanny McCullough

Executive Mansion,
Dear Fanny   Washington, December 23, 1862.

It is with deep grief that I learn of the death of your kind and brave Father; and, especially, that it is affecting your young heart beyond what is common in such cases. In this sad world of ours, sorrow comes to all; and, to the young, it comes with bitterest agony, because it takes them unawares. The older have learned to ever expect it. I am anxious to afford some alleviation of your present distress. Perfect relief is not possible, except with time. You can not now realize that you will ever feel better. Is not this so? And yet it is a mistake. You are sure to be happy again. To know this, which is certainly true, will make you some less miserable now. I have had experience enough to know what I say; and you need only to believe it, to feel better at once. The memory of your dear Father, instead of an agony, will yet be a sad sweet feeling in your heart, of a purer, and holier sort than you have known before.

Please present my kind regards to your afflicted mother.

Your sincere friend,
Abraham Lincoln

Lieutenant Colonel William McCullough, former clerk of county court in Bloomington, was a close acquaintance of Lincoln. He was killed in action on December 5, 1862.

Lincoln's Star

On the night of Good Friday, 1865, he left us to join a blessed procession, in neither doubt nor fear, but his soul does indeed go marching on. For this was the Bible-reading lad come out of wilderness, following a prairie star, filled with wonder at the world and its Maker, who all his life, boy and man, not only knew the Twenty-third Psalm, but more importantly, knew the Shepherd.

Everett McKinley Dirksen

Eve of a New Era

I feel that we are on the eve of a new era, when there is to be great harmony between the Federal and Confederate. I cannot stay to be a living witness to the correctness of this prophecy; but I feel it within me that it is to be so. The universally kind feeling expressed for me at a time when it was supposed that each day would prove my last, seemed to me the beginning of the answer to "Let us have peace."

Ulysses S. Grant

The Prospect for Peace, 1917

I am not surprised that one fails to understand the proposition which I tried to present, for it seems that a great many of our preachers do not understand it. I quoted to him from the New Testament where Christ said, "Love your enemies," and pointed out to him that love comes before justice—is, in fact, necessary to the understanding of justice. It is easy to love those who are good to us. It is to love those who despitefully use us that tests our religion.

The nations of Europe all contend that they are fighting for justice and that when they establish justice, friendship will follow. That is, in my opinion, the delusion that has kept the world at war, and will continue to make permanent peace impossible as long as the philosophy is followed.

As long as there is hatred in the heart, one cannot understand what justice is. If I understand our religion, love is presented as the greatest compelling force and forgiveness as its manifestation. The President's appeal to the nations to come together in a peace without victory was rejected by both sides because European governments are not built upon that theory, and now we are asked to enter into the war on the European plan.

If preachers who have dedicated their lives to the interpretation of the Gospel can see no higher standard of honor than the standard of war, it is hard to expect a man from Belgium whose heart is bleeding for his countrymen to be dispassionate enough to understand the philosophy of love and the fruit it is expected to produce.

William Jennings Bryan

Christmas in the Lincoln White House
by Julia Taft Bayne

Saturday morning, at our house, was devoted to a study of the Sunday school lesson. Willie and Tad appeared early, as they always did. The Lincoln boys had enrolled themselves with my brothers in the Sunday school of our church, the Fourth Presbyterian.

It was December and cold. Willie and Tad had been talking of winters in Illinois, of skating and sledding and snowballing. My

Washington-bred brothers listened with round eyes. They possessed no mittens, no sled, no skates. They had never known the delights of a real snowstorm.

Tad dashed at the Sabbath questions with the cheerful audacity characteristic of him. Willie sighed as he said that there were more hard words than ever in it.

The very youngest son of the family, Willie Taft, being what Tad called a "Sunday-school infant" and not required to study any lesson, sat curled up on the window seat.

The older boys studied with set, determined looks. There were several bits of catechism deftly interpolated; and in our Sunday school these must be recited verbatim. Tad and Holly wriggled and fidgeted, repeating the lines in a loud whisper, each gradually departing from the text and copying the other's mistakes until they had to begin all over again.

The infant scholar in the window also diverted attention by proclaiming at intervals. "There's a dwunk man walking the beat with a log," or "Here comes the officer of the day; they're turning out the guard." Again it would be, "I fink there's a hundred Army mules up the street fighting right smart."

Tad paused in the murmur of "the moral law—the moral law—" to ask, "Julie, what is a mud sill?"

"Never mind, Tad, go on. 'The moral law is summarily comprehended—'"

"But, what is it?"

"Why, a Yankee, Tad."

"Well, a boy in Lafayette Square said we were 'em, and we am not."

"Of course not," said Willie Lincoln. "Everybody knows they come from Connecticut."

"Bud and Willie wouldn't let me punch him 'cause they said it would be put in the papers, but I will if he says it again."

It was still cold and wet and blustering. Only an occasional officer rode past, his great cape over his head. The boys watched the gusts of rain anxiously. They had been promised a ride with the staff if it was not too stormy.

My cousin, a tall young captain . . . came and leaned against the doorway and sympathetically confessed that he himself had to learn the Commandments and Creed before the morrow's morn.

"What for?" demanded the boys, astonished that the shoulder-strapped six-footer should still be in thralldom to the blue question book.

"Because we have a Sunday school in the defenses, and the colonel is superintendent."

"Snow! snow!" shouted Tad, as some light flakes flew by the window. "That's what I like better'n anything. I hope it'll be over the fences."

Tad's wish was futile. To his great disappointment the snow-flakes grew more and more infrequent, and at last the sun shone out. The boys went off, hopeful of a ride at least.

About noon a relative arrived unexpectedly. As he had to go to his command that evening and wished to see the children, I was sent to find the boys and bring them home. I went at once to the White House and looked outside first; the grounds, the stable, the conservatory; then the kitchen, where I learned that the boys had an early lunch and had not been seen since. The ride with the staff had not materialized, and the Madam had gone for a drive but had not taken the boys.

I ran up into the sitting room and almost collided with the tall form of the President, who was crossing the room on the way to his office. He had some papers in one hand and with the other he stopped my flight, saying, "Here, here, flibbertigibbet, where are you going in such a hurry?"

"I am looking for the boys and I cannot find them anywhere. Cousin Sam Andrus is at our house with a colonel. I forget his name but he is awfully nice."

"Awfully nice, is he?" said Mr. Lincoln, with the quizzical smile I remember so well.

"Yes, sir, and they want to see the boys, ours and yours. Willie and Tad, you know."

"Yes, I know. Have you looked in the attic, Julie?"

"I'm going there now," I said, and left him watching my head-long progress toward the attic, with that same smile on his face.

In the attic was a large bin of visiting cards, which apparently had been lately distrubed, as there was a nest hollowed out in the center, and the cards were scattered all around the floor. But the boys were not there; so I went home and reported.

After dinner, as the men were enjoying their cigars . . . the four boys appeared, dragging an old chair on barrel staves and the cover of a Congressional Record nailed to the broken seat. This, they proudly informed us, was a snow sled.

Holly hung back as they were severally presented to the colonel, and Tad triumphantly explained that "Holly burned an awful hole in his pants with powder out of a cartridge given him by a soldier who said it wouldn't go off."

Both Tad and Holly were very uneasy and continually rubbed against the veranda railing. When questioned by mother, Tad said, "I s'pose it's the snowballs we've got down our backs."

"Snowballs," said mother, surprised. "Where did you find any snow?"

"Up in our attic," said Tad. "Handfuls and handfuls and bushels and bushels."

Naturally we all looked amazed at this statement until Willie explained. "Why, Mama Taft, Tad's snow is cards. There are bushels in our attic in a big bin and we throw them up and play it's snowing. There are all the cards all the people have left on the Presidents since General Washington."

"General Washington never lived in your house," said Bud. "The tutor said he didn't."

"Well, there's enough to make a snowstorm without his," said Willie.

"And Tad and Holly stuffed them down each other's backs like real snow, but I guess they're sharp cornered and sticky."

"Yes," said Tad; "they stick to you, and they stick into you."

Declaring they couldn't stand it another minute, Holly and Tad went upstairs, Tad calling back, "Next time we'll pour the snow on the attic stairs and slide down on our snow sled."

The next morning, going into the boys' room, I saw in the middle of the card-strewn floor the name of Jenny Lind, the great singer. So I picked up this card, and then another and another, as they interested me, leaving many to be swept up by the maid.

Some of the other snowflakes from Tad Lincoln's snowstorm were Horace Mann, Comm. Morris, Mrs. Jefferson Davis, Marquis de LaFayette.

Penny Letters

Because of the distance and difficulty of the trip most immigrants coming to this country in the 19th century did so knowing they would not be able to return. Letters were the sole means of keeping in touch, remembering relatives and friends at home. Post offices in towns, throughout Illinois in the 1860s, particularly at Christmas, advertised letters for new arrivals who had not obtained permanent residency. The following advertisement appeared in one Illinois newspaper in 1862.

Individuals receiving letters for week of December 15-22:

B.F. Felt
Gottleib Engels
N. Stillman

James O'Halloran
Eliza Hill
Thomas McFeeley

A charge of one cent is made on advertised letters which must be paid before the letter can be disbursed.

I'm bidding farewell to the
  land of my birth
To wander far over the sea
I am parting from all I hold
  dear on earth
Oh, it's breaking my poor
  heart will be

Irish-American Folk Song, Joseph Murphy

Christmases Past Remembered at Mr. Dooley's Bar
by Finley Peter Dunne

There was a turkey raffle on Halsted Street last night and Mr. McKenna shook forty-four. He came into Mr. Dooley's with the turkey under his arm and Mr. Dooley, who was mixing a Tom-and-Jerry dope on the end of the bar, paused to inquire, "Where'd ye get th' reed burrd, Jawnny?"

"I won it at Donnelly's raffle," said Mr. McKenna.

"Ye ought to 've kep' it in a warm place," said Mr. Dooley. "It's shrinkin' so 'twill be a fishball befure ye get home. It must be a canned turkey. I've seen th' likes of that in th' ol' counthry f'r ivrybody that cud get thim wanted turkey f'r Chris'mas an' if they cuddent get a big fat gobbler with meat enough on him to feed a rigmint of Mayo min they took what they got, an' they got wan of thim little herrin' turkeys like th' burrd ye have under ye'er ar-rm. Faith, it wasn't all of thim cud get that much, poor things! There was places in th' pa-art of Ireland ye'er people come fr'm, Jawn, with ye'er di'mons an' ye'er gol'headed umbrellas, where a piece of bacon an' an exthra allowance of pitaties was a feast f'r th' kids. 'Twas in ye'er town, Jawn, that th' little girl, whin she wanted to remimber something, says to th' ol' man; 'Why,' she says, 'ye remimber 'twas th' day we had meat, says she.. She remembered it because 'twas th' day they had meat, Jawn. 'Twas like Christmas an' th' Foorth of July an' Pathrick's day, whin they had meat in ye'er part of Ireland, Jawn. On other occasions they had pitaties an' butthermilk, or, if their neighbors wuz kind, oatmeal stirabout. Poor things! Did I iver tell ye about me Uncle Clarence that died of overatin' reed burrds?"

"You did," said Mr. McKenna surlily, for it was a point upon which Mr. Dooley often jibed him.

"Annyhow," said Mr. Dooley, grinning, "poor or rich alike, th' people of Ireland never let th' Christmas pass without cellybratin'. Ye'd know th' day was comin' frim th' gr-reat coortin' that'd be goin' on ivrywhere. Advint week was always gr'reat coortin' time f'r th' la-ads. They'd make love befure Christmas an' get married aftherward if th' gir'rls 'd have thim an' they mostly would. That's a way th' gir-rls have th' whole wur-ruld over.

"Thin ivery man 'd wish f'r a snowy Chris'mas. A green

Chris'mas makes a fat churchyard, says th' good book, an' like as not there'd be snow on th' ground, at laste in Maynooth where I come fr'm. An' about Chris'mas eve th' lads an' lasses 'd go into th' hills an' fetch down ivy to hang above th' hearth an' all th' kids 'd go light on th' stirabout so's they could tuck in more on th' morrow. Chris'mas eve th' lads that'd been away 'd come thrampin' in from Gawd knows where, big lads far fr'm home in Cork an' Limerick an' th' City of Dublin—come thrampin' home stick in hand to ate their Chris'mas dinner with th' ol' folks. Dear, oh dear, how I remimber it. 'Twas a long road that led up to our house an' me mother'd put a lamp in th' windy so's th' la-ads could see th' way. Manny's th' time I've heerd th' beat of th' stick on th' road an' th' tap on th' pane an' me mother runnin' to th' dure an' screamin' Mike, 'r Tim, 'r Robert Immitt an' cryin' on his shoulder. 'Twas, let me see, four fours is sixteen, an' thirty makes forty-six—'twas in th' Christmas of fifty-sivin I last seen me brother Mike, poor fellow, poor fellow.

"We was up early, ye may say that, th' nex' mornin'. Some of th' pious wans 'd go to th' midnight mass an' thim we called 'voteens.' But th' kids had little thought of mass till they opened their Chris'mas boxes. Poor little Chris'mas boxes they was, like enough a bit of a dolly f'r th' little girls an' a Jack-in-the-box with whiskers like Postmaster Hesting's an' a stick of candy. There's on'y wan thing ye have over here that we niver had at home, an' that's Sandy Claus. Why is it, 'd'ye suppose? I never knew that St. Patrick druv him out with th' snakes, but I niver heerd of him till I come to this counthry.

"Thin afther th' Chris'mas boxes th' kids 'd go out in th' road an' holler 'Chris'mas box' at ivry man they met an' thin wud be off to mass where th' priest's niece sung th' 'Destah Fidelis,' an' ivry man chipped in a shillin' or two f'r th' good man. By gar, some of thim soggarths was bor-rn politicians, f'r they cud jolly a man f'r givin' big an' roast him f'r givin' a little till ivry citizen in th' parish was thryin' to beat his neighbor like as if 'twas at a game of give-away. Ye'd hear thim comin' home fr'm th' church. 'Th' iday of Mike Casey givin' tin shillin's whin Badalia Casey burrid a pinch of tay fr'm me on'y las' week.' 'What a poor lot thim Dugans is. Before I'd be read frim th' altar with six pince afther me name I'd sell th' shoes off me feet. I heerd Tim Dugan got three poun' tin f'r that litther of boneens. Did ye notice he wint to his jooty today. Faith, 'tis time. I was thinkin' he was goin' to join th' Prowtestants.'

"An' so 'twud go. Thin they was dinner, a hell of a dinner, of turkey, or goose with bacon an' thin a bottle of th' ol' shtuff with limon an' hot wather, an' toasts was drunk to th' la-ads far away an' to thim in prison an' to another reunion an' late at night me mother 'd tuck us all in bed an' lade me father to his room with his jag upon him singin' 'Th' Wearin' of th' Green' at th' top of his voice. Thim ol' days!"

"Well, Martin, good night," said McKenna. "A merry Christmas before I see you again."

"Merry Christmas," said Mr. Dooley. If Mr. McKenna had returned five minutes later he would have found Mr. Dooley sitting on the edge of the bed in the back room wiping his eyes on the bar towel.

Turn of the century Chicago journalist and humorist Finley Peter Dunne created "Mr. Dooley," the Irish-American saloon keeper whose amusing comments satirized current events.

Christmas at Hull House

by Hilda Sutt Polacheck

Several days before Christmas 1896 one of my Irish playmates suggested that I go with her to a Christmas party at Hull-House. I told her that I never went to Christmas parties.

"Why not?" she asked.

"I do not go anywhere on Christmas Day," I said.

"But this party will not be on Christmas Day. It will be the Sunday before Christmas Day," she said.

I repeated that I could not go and she persisted in wanting to know why. Before I could think, I blurted out the words: "I might get killed."

"Get killed!" She stared at me. "I go to Hull-House Christmas parties every year, and no one was ever killed."

I then asked her if there would be any Jewish children at the party. She assured me that there had been Jewish children at the parties every year and that no one was ever hurt.

The thought began to percolate through my head that things might be different in America. In Poland it had not been safe for Jewish children to be on the streets on Christmas. I struggled with my conscience and finally decided to accompany my friend to the Hull-House Christmas party. This was the second time that I was doing something without telling Mother.

My friend and I arrived at Hull-House and went to the coffee shop where the party was being held. There were many children and their parents seated when we arrived. It was the first time that I had sat in a room where there was a Christmas tree. In fact, there were two trees in the room: one on each side of the high brick fireplace. The trees looked as if they had just been brought in from a heavy snowstorm. The glistening glass icicles and asbestos snow looked very real. The trees were lighted with white candles and on each side stood a man with a pail of water and a mop, ready to put out any accidental fire.

People called to each other across the room. Then I noticed that I could not understand what they were saying. It dawned on me that the people in this room had come from other countries. Yet there was no tension. Everybody seemed to be having a good time. There were children and parents at this party from Russia,

Poland, Italy, Germany, Ireland, England, and many other lands, but no one seemed to care where they had come from, or what religion they professed, or what clothes they wore, or what they thought. As I sat there, I am sure I felt myself being freed from a variety of century-old superstitions and inhibitions. There seemed to be nothing to be afraid of.

Then Jane Addams came into the room! It was the first time that I looked into those kind, understanding eyes. There was a gleam of welcome in them that made me feel I was wanted. She told us that she was glad we had come. Her voice was warm and I knew she meant what she said. She was the second person who made me glad that I had come to America. Mrs. Torrance was the first.

The children of the Hull-House Music School then sang some songs, that I later found out were called "Christmas carols." I shall never forget the caressing sweetness of those childish voices. All feelings of religious intolerance and bigotry faded. I could not connect this beautiful party with any hatred or superstition that existed among the people of Poland.

As I look back, I know that I became a staunch American at this party. I was with children who had been brought here from all over the world. The fathers and mothers, like my father and mother, had come in search of a free and happy life. And we were all having a good time at a party, as the guests of an American, Jane Addams.

We were all poor. Some of us were underfed. Some of us had holes in our shoes. But we were not afraid of each other. What greater service can a human being give to her country than to banish fear from the heart of a child? Jane Addams did that for me at that party.

While I felt that I had done nothing wrong or sinful by going to the Christmas party, I still hesitated telling Mother where I had been. I was glad that she did not ask me.

Christmas in Bavarian Heaven
by Carl B. Roden

Once upon a time [never mind how long ago] in that section of the old north side of Chicago called *Bayerischer Himmel*—Bavarian Heaven—there stood a two-story frame house owned by our uncle, who lived upstairs, and inhabited below by "us." German was the speech of the household and was almost as common on the street as English. One went to a little German school three doors away, and did not feel the lack of English until one changed to public school and for a little while had trouble in getting on. During the Chicago Fire not many years before [never mind how many], the family silver and the huge square piano had been buried in the back yard while the family fled to a farmer friend out in the country, at Fullerton and Racine Avenues.

But now the silver was in service again, and the big piano tinkled merrily under the fleet fingers of our gifted aunt, especially at Christmas. For she knew all the German Christmas songs: *Stille Nacht, Ihr Kinderlein kommet, O Tannebaum* and the rest. Thus, with music from above and with flavorsome baking and cooking in our own kitchen, the Christmas mood was established, the season ushered in by a visit from a grim St. Nicholas bearing nuts and apples for good children and rods for the backs of the bad.

And, when the Day dawned—and our Christmas was always in the morning—there was the tree with its sputtering candles [not bulbs], the waxen angels and the other seasonal accouterments. Below were the gifts, not mysteriously wrapped but out in the open, to be claimed and envied and perhaps fought over. Our gifts came mostly from North Avenue, where they didn't cost too much. For that matter, we rarely went down town which was pretty far away; nearly three miles on a horse car. Once in a while there would be an "expensive" gift from Schweitzer and Beer's, that wondrous emporium of toys on State street at Monroe. It would probably be a musical instrument or a book. In particular, I remember a gorgeous book called Fata Morgana, a retelling of the Arabian Nights, with beautiful colored illustrations that, when held to the light, revealed the very witch or fairy about whom the tale was told. And I remember many other things about those Christmases, all beautiful and marvelous.

But one year we moved away from all this, the family to far Lake View, and ourselves into a new decade of life. In June of that year President Garfield was shot by a lunatic and died in September. And that's how long ago all this was!

Among the special memories of Christmas was the aroma-filled kitchen that indicated that our mother was preparing our Christmas "goodies"—Lebkuchen, pferrernusse, and especially kaffeekuchen, of which mother made enough to last for the whole season (at least, so it seemed to me).

Sister Mary Ursula, Alton

Kaffee Kuchen

1/4 c. milk	1/4 c. warm water
1/4 c. sugar	1 pkg. active dry yeast
1/2 tsp. salt	1 egg, beaten
3 Tbsp. butter or margarine	2-1/4 c. sifted all-purpose flour

In a small saucepan, scald milk (heat until bubbles form around the edge of the pan); remove from heat and add sugar, salt, and butter and stir until butter is melted. Let this mixture cool until lukewarm. In the meantime dissolve yeast in warm water; add to milk mixture only when it has cooled. Add egg and 1-1/2 c. flour; beat with wooden spoon until smooth. Add rest of flour and mix until dough leaves the side of bowl. Turn out dough on lightly floured surface; knead until dough is satiny and elastic and blisters appear on surface. Place in lightly greased large bowl; cover with damp towel and let rise in a warm place until double in bulk, one to one and a half hours. Punch down dough with fist and return to floured surface; knead 10 to 15 times. Roll into a 32″ x 8″ strip. Brush with 1 Tbsp. melted butter and add a filling. The filling can be many things: 1/2 cup of cherry or apple canned pie filling; a mixture of 1/4 c. brown sugar, 1 Tbsp. soft butter, 1 tsp. cinnamon; canned poppy seed filling; a mixture of 1/4 c. each chopped almonds and raisins, and soft butter spread on dough then sprinkled with 1 tsp. cinnamon, 2 Tbsp. sugar. Roll dough from long side, forming a long rope. Pinch edges and end to seal well. Spiral rope into a tube pan, beginning in center of pan. Cover with damp towel and let rise again until double in size. Meanwhile, preheat oven to 350°, bake for 25-35 minutes, until browned. Remove from pan and cool on wire rack. Glaze top with an icing of 1/2 c. powdered sugar, 1 Tbsp. milk, 1/4 tsp. vanilla extract. May be frozen when completely cool.

A Swedish Celebration

by Gloria Jahoda

Christmas in Chicago! To me it is the Christmas of Belmont and Sheffield avenues ("Wheffield," Chicago's Swedes used to call it). In my childhood this was the center of Chicago's Swedish life, of which I was a part. I can still see the street lights there, the thin snowflakes whirling about them at dusk. I see wet windowpanes thru which herring barrels and lingonberry jars in Otto Johnson's fish market loomed large and wavy sided and tantalizing.

The marquee of the Julian theater blinked its announcement of Swedish holiday movies, and the stationery stores were full of cards which carried Swedish messages of *"Göd Jul!"* and bright pictures of costumed peasant girls.

I stand again in memory in Hannah Persson's bakery. I smell its unbelievable clouds of fragrance: hot saffron bread and sculptured pastries, wild blueberry jelly tarts, the ginger cookies called *pepparkokar*. Hannah waits behind her counter with a handful of red striped white mints, *polkagriser*, and she smiles to me: "These I find for you."

The celebration still begins for me on Swedish Saint Lucia day, December 13. Our family began it then in Chicago. One year I was Saint Lucia, in long white robes, crowned with a circle of candles to serve cookies.

Our tree was always up by Saint Lucia day, and as we decorated it with golden pears and silver grapes we sang the Saint Lucia song: "Christmas is here again, and Christmas lasts till Easter!" Then we joined hands in a ring as my father turned on the lights.

My mother began the verses of Frithiof's saga every Chicago Swede knew by heart:

> *King Ring sat on his throne.*
> *Drinking his Christmas mead;*
> *Beside him sat his Queen,*
> *So white and rosy red. . . .*

And on Christmas Eve when I was old enough to stay up I first heard the sound I hope my heart will hear as long as I live: the soft footsteps of Swedish families on packed snow as they walked in darkness, single candles in their hands, to the city's Julotta services which ushered in the Christmas dawn.

Pepparkakor

2/3 cup brown or ordinary sugar
2/3 c. molasses
1 tsp. ginger
1 tsp. cinnamon
1/2 tsp. cloves

3/4 Tbsp. baking soda
2/3 c. butter
1 egg
5 c. flour

Heat sugar, molasses and spices to boiling point. Add baking soda and pour mixture over butter in bowl. Stir until butter melts. Add egg and sifted flour and blend thoroughly. Knead on baking board. Chill. Roll out and cut with fancy cutters (at Christmas into Santa Claus shapes, Christmas trees, animal forms, etc.). Place on greased baking sheet and bake in slow to moderate oven (325° F.) 8-10 minutes.

Py Jimminey, I vas wishin' you
all sorts of Goot Times
und Happiness
fur Xmas

Polkagrisar

1 lb. sugar
1 c. water
1 Tbsp. dextrose

2 tsp. vinegar
3 drops peppermint oil
red coloring

Mix sugar, dextrose, water and vinegar in saucepan and let stand until dissolved. Bring quickly to boil and cook over low heat (275° F.) or until mixture becomes brittle when dropped in cold water. Remove from heat and allow to cool 3-4 minutes. Pour 3/4 onto oiled baking sheet. Add peppermint and turn edges constantly towards middle with spatula. When cold enough to handle, stretch with oiled hands. Fold, stretch and fold continuously. Then pull into one long strip and place on oiled baking sheet. Color remaining candy red and pour onto baking sheet in two strips, one on either side of white candy. Twist strips together and cut immediately with oiled scissors into different shapes.

In accordance with the usual custom, the First Methodist church had a Christmas tree; not a small ordinary affair, but a monster tree, its huge branches nearly covering the large platform, and capable of supporting a multitude of gifts; . . . from the base to summit it was beautifully set with long strings of popcorn, mingled in good taste with colored balls and sparkling ornaments of various kinds; and, to add to the general pleasing effect, it was brilliantly lighted with small wax tapers. Then, there was Santa Claus—a real live St. Nick,—who was dressed in a loose shift of white clothes, covered with spangles from head to foot, and whose huge beard almost hid his smiling face.

Champaign County Gazette, December 27, 1893

The finest Christmas tree in the city, was that prepared for the children, by the Sisters of St. Mary's Catholic Church. It was a symmetrical evergreen, some twelve feet in height, and presented a gorgeous picture with its load of gifts and glistening tapers. The tree was exhibited in the school building back of the church, immediately after First Mass on Christmas morning, and hundreds of children, gathered about it, gazing admiringly and longingly into its branches.

Galena Weekly Gazette, December 31, 1880

The Christmas Tree Ship
by Harry Hansen

Christmas in Chicago, fifty years ago, was a happy, home festival in a city not yet too rich, too pretentious, to be neighborly. There was usually snow at Christmas; it lay in large heaps in the gutters and was packed solid on the streets. When snow fell it was heavy with moisture; it blocked trains and held up streetcars. The average citizen shoveled his own sidewalks clean and looked after his own fires. A few blocks beyond the Loop, where the gray wooden cottages with their scrollwork porches stretched for miles, householders would be out early in the mornings wielding their shovels, amid shouts to their neighbors, for in those days families lived long enough in one locality to become known to one another.

In the houses on the near North Side, where brick buildings abounded, the windows had little wooden blinds inside through which came the yellow rays of light from gas jets. The air in the streets outside had the close feeling of a low-ceilinged room and shouts rebounded from wall to wall. In that air bells on sleighs jingled in time a long way off and hoofbeats made a dull patter on the packed snow. As the sleigh passed under the light of the gas lamp at the corner you could see the prancing horse, the curved dashboard, the gleam of the nickeled bars across the front, the flash of the runners. The driver would be wearing a wide fur collar and a fur cap; the woman beside him would be tucked under fur robes and look very comfortable in a brown fur neckpiece and toque.

Inside, the house was warm and a bit stuffy with dry air. The carpets had a firm surface and gay curlicues of vine leaves all over them. The hall might be dark; its walls were covered with embossed paper, stained to the color of leather, and the gaslight flickered behind a globe of pink glass ornamented with a trailing vine. You walked quickly past the parlor, which had a mantelpiece of black slate and a mirror over the fireplace and heavy chairs and settees with curved walnut legs, to the back room where all the family gathered. Here the walls were hung with photographs of young and old and there were music racks and bookshelves. If the house was heated by a furnace, the hot air flooded up through a register in the floor, but more likely a big-bellied stove, consuming anthracite coal, gleamed red through mica windows in a corner. And in the bay stood the Christmas tree.

Most likely the father of the family had picked it out and carried it home. Men and women carried their own bundles in those days. Perhaps he walked down to the Clark Street Bridge, a week or two before Christmas, to see if the Schuenemanns had come down from Wisconsin with a load of spruce trees. Invariably the two big, brawny lads would be there with a fishing schooner loaded with trees that they themselves had cut in the Michigan woods. They were fine, well-shaped trees and cost so little—for 75 cents you bought a fullsized tree; for $1 you had your choice of the best. Even saplings provided bright decorations for a city where people were making money, but not too much money, and where the average citizen was always fearful of hard times.

As long ago as 1887 the two Schuenemanns, Herman and August, had sailed down in a schooner from Manistique, Michigan, with a load of spruce and tied up beside the dock behind the old red-brick commission houses at the Clark Street bridge. There Chicago found them and bought their stock, and called Herman captain and remembered to look for him the following year. When snow fell on Chicago's streets in December days the father of the family would say, "Guess I'll have to go down to the Clark Street bridge to see if the captain is in and get us a tree."

Fifty years ago the work of providing trees for Christmas was not yet the mass-production business it has become in recent times. No dealer contracted for thousands of trees as a speculation and destroyed great numbers if he had guessed wrong on the demand. No man cut down whole hillsides to satisfy the whims of people who followed a custom but didn't know how to pray. There were plenty of trees for all. The Schuenemanns went into the woods behind Manistique and Thompson, Michigan, where young trees grew on land that had been cut over to make the lumber that went into midwestern houses a generation before. They chose the trees carefully, including some tall ones for which they had orders from churches and hotels. Sometimes they had to work in the snow and when the trees reached Chicago there was still snow on the branches. The brothers thought they had done well when they made a modest profit on a trip that occupied about six weeks of the wintry season, when it was hard to haul other cargoes.

The work was not easy, neither the cutting nor the sailing, for they always came when Lake Michigan kicked up a lot of rough sea. In 1898 August had just set sail with a load of trees when a storm arose and he and his ship were lost. Thereupon Herman determined to carry on alone. In 1899 he was back at the Clark Street dock with his boat, the *Rouse Simmons*, loaded with Christmas trees. He was a jovial man, with a very ruddy complexion and laughing wrinkles around his blue eyes, and everybody liked him.

For eleven years Herman arrived with his cargo and many people depended on him for a tree year after year. Then came the hard season of 1912, with storms and heavy seas on Lake Michigan. Late in November Herman cut his trees in the woods behind Manistique and started for Chicago in the *Rouse Simmons*, with a crew of seventeen men. There were head winds and heavy seas from the start and soon the schooner was struggling in a raging snowstorm. What took place on board we can only guess. The *Rouse Simmons* sailed into the silence that covers all the fine ships that have fallen victim to the gales of Lake Michigan, which have taken the lives of so many, from the days of La Salle's *Griffon* until now.

Long before Chicago missed the *Rouse Simmons* at its dock reports began to come of the ship's distress. A schooner resembling it was said to have been sighted off Kewaunee, Wisconsin, flying distress signals. The steamer *George W. Orr* reported to the revenue cutter *Tuscarora* that she had seen the *Rouse Simmons* three miles offshore, but the captain later admitted that he might have been mistaken. But on December 5, 1912, fishermen off Two Rivers Point, seven miles north of Manitowoc, Wisconsin, found the tops of spruce trees entangled in their nets. Trees had been roped together on the deck of the *Rouse Simmons*, and how could they get into the lake at that point if not off a ship?

On December 13th a watcher on the beach at Sheboygan, Wisconsin, reported that he had picked up a bottle containing a message that came from the captain. It had been written on a page of the ship's log and read:

Friday—Everybody goodbye. I guess we are all through. Sea washed over our deckload Thursday. During the night the small boat was washed over. Leaking bad. Ingvald and Steve fell overboard Thursday. God help us.

Herman Schuenemann

The men referred to were believed to have been Steve E. Nelson, mate, and Ingvald Nylons, seaman. But if there was such a message, it never reached the captain's wife, who was eagerly waiting for scraps of news in her Manistique home. She was a valiant little woman, with a great deal of stamina. When she realized that her three little girls, Elsie and the twins, Pearl and Hazel, were now dependent wholly on her efforts, she resolved to take up her husband's task.

There was no Christmas ship at the Clark Street dock in 1912. But when 1913 came, Chicago residents who looked over the railings of the bridge behld another schooner, loaded with trees, as in the days when Captain Herman held forth there. On board was the plucky little wife of the captain. She had gone into the woods with the woodcutters and supervised the felling of the trees. With her, too, were her girls, as well as women to weave wreaths and garlands. Chicago was to become well acquainted with the Schuenemanns. They were to come season after season for twenty-two years after the *Rouse Simmons* went down.

It's Good to Be Black

by Ruby Berkley Goodwin

Usually Dad was the first one up to start the fires, but not so on Christmas morning. Even before daybreak, curiosity had chased the sleep from our eyes. A whispered "See anything?" came from near the bedroom door. I answered back a negative "uh-uh!" Spud crept to the center of the room near the base-burner. I slid out of bed. Together we tiptoed about the room. Helen slept soundly as did the smaller children in the next room.

Through the semi-darkness we could see long-ribbed cotton stockings, knotted with Oregon apples and Florida oranges, hanging about on the walls, like stumpy chicken snakes full of eggs. A small table near the south wall held cereal bowls of Christmas candy shaped like bows and rosettes. There were chocolate drops and creamy white sticks with intricate colored designs running through the center. Pecans, almonds, Brazil and English walnuts were mixed with the hickory nuts and scaly-barks we had gathered in the fall on the banks of Big Muddy Creek.

Spud shook down the ashes and soon had a roaring fire in the base-burner. The younger children were now awake, and as they crowded about the pile of gaily wrapped presents on the floor they glanced impatiently toward the bedroom where Mother lay. Dad hushed their inquiries with a simple statement, "Your mother don't feel so well this morning." Immediately, we became silent and unconsciously grouped ourselves in the bedroom door. We had forgotten the presents and the Christmas goodies in our anxiety.

Whether Aunt Dea was sent for or just happened to drop in, we never knew. Somehow she was there, nudging toys and young ones gently aside with her foot, sashaying into the bedroom with a steaming cup of tea, and stuffing a twenty-pound turkey Mother's brother Sargeant had sent her from California. Under her clipped commands and searching eyes the folding bed in the living room became a davenport, ashes were brushed from the faded floral rug, chairs were pushed against the walls, lamps were filled, and chimneys were polished. The pungent smell of celery, onions, garlic, and sage filled the four rooms and slipped quietly outside where it hung about the porches in the crisp December air.

It was early afternoon when Aunt Dea, after numerous trips

into Mother's room, came back into the kitchen and sent Helen and me to call Dr. Gillis.

"Hit the grit!" she ordered. 'And don't stop to talk." With Aunt Dea, a doctor was the last resort. This may have been due to the heavy strain of Indian blood that fought for domination over her Negroid heritage. She was tall and angular, and so marked were her Indian features that a band of Cherokees who once came to town with Buffalo Bill followed her home, grunting gibberish to her all the way. We knew her trusted remedies, sugar and turpentine for stomach-ache or cramps, onion syrup for coughs, jimson weeds dampened and tied on the forehead for headache, and red pepper and corn meal poultices for pneumonia. When Aunt Dea didn't trust these, the patient was mighty sick.

We pulled on our fleece-lined overshoes, buttoned our heavy coats about our throats, and tied woolen fascinators under our chins.

Dr. Gillis and sickness were synonymous, and the former usually arrived just a jump or so behind the latter. Even if the bony finger of death had rapped on the window and beckoned for you to follow, Dr. Gillis had only to poke his shiny head in the door to send the grim monster packing.

As Helen and I hurried along, I thought of a remark Dad had made. "He's something like the Lord. Any time you call Dr. Gillis, he'll come." We ran every step of the way, the deep snow clinging and pulling us back as we lifted our feet from the heavy drifts. We were out of breath when we reached the gashouse where the only phone in our part of town hung in a smoky little aperture on the wall. Coming from the dazzling whiteness outside, the interior of the plant was dismal. The red glow from the open door of the furnace cast an eerie light over the half-bent solitary figure at the other end of the building.

"Can we use your phone, Simon?" I called.

Simon, slim, black, and perspiring in spite of the zero weather outside, stopped scooping the shovelsful of nut coal, mopped his brow with a large bandana, and answered, "Sho, sho. How's Mis' Sophia?"

"She ain't so good. Aunt Dea sent us to call Dr. Gillis." Even as I answered Simon I was turning the crank and listening for the voice of the operator. Simon's eyes took on the glare of the furnace as he stood within the circle of its light, resting himself on the handle of the shovel.

Despite the frequency of childbirth in our household, we had never associated anything painful or unpleasant with it. Mother was a Spartan, and there was never an outcry or a moan. As we grew older however, we became apprehensive for we remembered Mrs. McLemore, who never walked another step after Lora was born. Then there was the young wife, Lilly Rivers, who never lived to see her baby. Her cries of pain were choked by the death rattle in her throat.

Dr. Gillis' voice boomed at me through the receiver, and suddenly the words I wanted to say knotted in my throat. Helen looked at me anxiously, her small round face catching the edge of my own terror. "Hello, hello," said the impatient voice. I'm going to fail Mother, I thought. I'm going to stand here like a rock and Dr. Gillis is going to hang up, and a terrible darkness will sweep over the counterpane with Mother's face showing over the edge of it.

Then, miraculously, the urgency came rising up in me and I was answering Dr. Gillis with a thin, quavering voice.

"This is Ruby Berkley, Dr. Gillis. It's Mama's time," I kept saying, "It's Mama's time." I was still holding the cold black instrument in my hand after Dr. Gillis had finished his mutterings about a kettle of fish, plenty of hot water, and coming as soon as he could get there.

We lifted our feet high as we walked across the vacant corner lot, pausing to catch our breath and look at the familiar landscape. The dwellings of the miners and the pretentious homes of the operators and merchants were softened by the snow that blanketed the town with its ermine whiteness. Rimmed by the broad acres of farm land, the tipple houses above the mines were not unlike slender church spires.

Dad had evidently been watching, for as we started around the house the front door opened and he called to us. His face, the color of unpolished old bronze, was filled with apprehension. When he knew that Dr. Gillis was on his way, some of the lines disappeared. He smiled a little, showing strong, even mother-of-pearl teeth. With his right hand he absent-mindedly stroked the heavy mustache that almost hid his upper lip.

Mother's bed which was usually flush against the east wall had been pulled out. Aunt Dea was busy smoothing out several thicknesses of a worn sheet blanket beneath her. A red velvet motto, "God Bless Our Home," hung by a silk cord on the wall above the bed.

Mother's smile was wan and detached. I asked her if I could get something for her. She shook her head, and for the first time I noticed the small beads of perspiration that stood out on her forehead. The heavy reversible spread she had bought from an Italian peddler was carefully folded back and made a colorful strip across the foot of the bed. Her hands gripped the nine-patch quilt of gingham blocks that lay across her full breast.

"Don't be botherin' yore ma with foolish questions. Git!" Aunt Dea started us from the room with a wave of her hand. As I turned to go, I noticed a pair of scissors someone had carelessly left on the bed. I reached back and picked them up, this time addressing my question to Aunt Dea. "You don't need these, do you?"

She looked up again. Her brown hand dropped the fold of the blanket and darted through the air like the hooded head of a cobra. She snatched the scissors from me fiercely and pushed them under the spread. "Leave 'em be," she hissed. "Something sharp on the bed—anything sharp—will help cut the birthing pains."

Back in the kitchen I picked up a paper-bound copy of *St. Elmo*, the then current best seller. The moody hero and pious Edna Earl were far from my mind. I put the book aside and went to the north window where Helen sat watching a group of boys playing snowballs. She had almost forgotten the matinee party she had been invited to and the dinner to follow at the farmhouse of Mr. Vincent, the only colored farmer who lived east of town. Those exciting, red-letter events had been pushed gently aside that morning by Dad's quiet understatement that Mother didn't feel well. Helen turned around addressing no one in particular. "Here's Dr. Gillis."

Aunt Dea came to the window, took one look and shouted, "What in God's world is the matter with Dr. Gillis?" To us, there was nothing strange about his actions. He was patting Cecil on the head, then carefully giving him the small black bag he had pulled from the seat of his car. Now he was striding up the cinder-strewn walk with Spud and Cecil on either side of him. Robert and the other boys were still standing by the car, some watching the trio as they advanced toward the house, others making faces at themselves in the shiny fenders or gliding their hands over the large convex headlights.

Aunt Dea, with a woman's eye for detail, had noticed the satin stripe down the trouser legs. Thin wisps of sandy hair peeked from beneath a high top hat. Instead of the practical Scotch-plaid muffler he usually wore, a most dressy silk-brocaded scarf was looped over and tucked beneath the lapels of his heavy black broadcloth topcoat.

At the door, Cecil gave the bag back to Dr. Gillis and he and Spud turned to rejoin their comrades. Dr. Gillis greeted us all by name as he entered the house. Both Aunt Dea and Dad towered over the short Scotch-Irishman. He walked into the bedroom and over to Mother's bed and smiled down at her as he reached back to give Aunt Dea his topcoat, scarf and hat. Then Helen and I noticed for the first time his formal cutaway coat, the white vest and the pleated stiff-bosom shirt with the pearl studs down the front. Aunt Dea was about to burst wide open with curiosity, but she said nothing as she folded the coat and scarf and carefully laid them on the boys' bed in the next room. She put the top hat on the dresser. A hat on the bed was bad luck and Aunt Dea was taking no chances. Mama needed all the good luck we could muster up for her. When Tom, who now toddled about the floor, was born, Dr. Gillis had told Mother and Dad there should be no more children. Aunt Dea and Aunt Ida had been saying that for years but Mother and Dad had paid them no mind.

Just as most children carry on the deception of a belief in Santa Claus for the benefit of their parents, so it was with our knowledge of birth. We had never been told the fascinating story of the birds and the bees. The extent of our sex education had been the rather casual admonition at about the age of thirteen to "keep your dress down." Nevertheless, we knew that germinating a new life was due to some sort of strange and mysterious rite legally reserved for married folks.

Activities in the bedroom seemed to speed up. Dr. Gillis had replaced the cutaway coat with his white surgeon's smock. Aunt Dea had put a few drops of a queer-smelling disinfectant in a basin of warm water and had held it while he washed his hands. The copper kettle on the back of the stove had been kept filled with boiling water. The steam had long since chased the frost from the windows.

Aunt Dea was kept busy between the kitchen and Mother's room. She tore ragged sheets, saved especially for this occasion, with a great ripping noise, and muttered to herself about the unfairness of a providence that made good women suffer while no-' count men got off scot-free. From time to time she basted the Christmas turkey, put out vegetables for us to prepare, or sent us on errands up to Aunt Ida's house.

Everyone in the neighborhood knew that Mother's time had come. Kate Seaman, a little German lady who lived directly north of us, came over with a steaming bowl of soup, "to giff 'er strent." But Mother was too busy for eating, and shortly after the door had closed behind Kate, a breathless, terrifying wail sounded through the house.

The crying stopped almost as quickly as it had begun. There were sounds of quick movements, clipped monosyllables, breathless silences. Then came the voice of Dr. Gillis weighted with good-natured scolding and intense relief. "Young lady," Dr. Gillis held the small bundle in his arms, "you sure played hell with Du Quoin society this afternoon. I'm supposed to be playing best man to Harry Miller and here I am tying your navel cord."

"Helen, it's a girl." I was slightly disappointed with Mother.

"Well, I'm glad. I'm tired of old long-headed boys." There had been seven boys in a row.

Presently, Aunt Dea came to the door and beckoned with her index finger. "Dr. Gillis said you could see your little sister now."

We went into the room. Dad was leaning over the bed, looking at something almost hidden in a downy pink and white blanket. He and Dr. Gillis were smiling as though they were well pleased with themselves. Mother's smile was different. It was weak but relaxed. Her eyes were tired but shining. I wanted to lean over and kiss her but I was shy, and contented myself with a peek at the baby before Helen nudged me out of the way so that she could get a better look.

The new baby was named Frances Ann for her two grandmothers. Dr. Gillis wrote the name on a small pad, returned the pad to his pocket and slid into a cane-bottom rocker.

"Sophia, I know you did all the work, but I'll be damned if

I'm not tired, too." He rested his elbow on the arm of the chair and covered his eyes with his hand. When he addressed Dad, he spoke softly as though speaking more to himself. "Braxton, you've got a fine family."

"I think so too, Doc. 'Course it's a poor dog that won't wag his own tail."

After a few minutes, Dr. Gillis stood and moved slowly about the room. He fitted the small vials and bottles into his bag, then pulled on his gloves. Dad held his topcoat. "How much is the bill, Doc?"

Dad reached in his pocket and handed Dr. Gillis two bills. "I'll catch up the slack in the next couple of paydays," he promised.

"Don't worry about me, Braxton. You've got too many mouths to feed. I'm not trying to get rich off of you. And don't think I'm sympathizing either. You're a millionaire." A thread of envy could be traced in Dr. Gillis's voice, for he and his wife were childless.

If Dad sensed the wistfulness he ignored it by saying, "Wish I could make 'em believe that millionaire stuff up at the company store when we're out on strike."

Dr. Gillis had reached the front door. He adjusted his silk hat and stepped out upon the porch. The snow on the walk had been packed hard by the tramping of many feet.

Christmas, always a day of delightful surprises, had outdone itself. Along with Roman Beauty apples, peppermint sticks, toys and dresses, it had brought us an olive-tinted baby, whose advent had delayed Du Quoin's most fashionable wedding for two whole hours.

Ruby Berkley Goodwin was born in the southern Illinois mining town of Du Quoin in 1903. She won prizes for poetry and published three books including a delightful autobiography from which this excerpt is taken.

From Main Street
to State Street

My Brother Adlai and Me

by Elizabeth Stevenson Ives

Adlai and I are the fifth generation of our family to live in Illinois, and there is no other place so close to our hearts. An Easterner friend said recently, "Whenever your brother says 'Illinois' he gives it such a special, loving sound that I find myself feeling wistful because I didn't grow up there."

The house on Washington Street is the home I came back to, with my husband Ernest Ives and our son Timothy, when Ernest retired after thirty years abroad in the Foreign Service. The ginkos, maples and chestnut trees Mother planted are now a high, leafy awning over the porch and lawn. As a girl back from boarding school, I exulted in my diary. "Home again! Home—the sweetest, freshest, greenest place in all the world!" Now that I've lived over a good bit of the world, I still feel that way. It has always seemed to me that the prairie sky is vaster and nearer to earth, and I get a sense of peaceful purpose and fulfillment from the rich, black, rolling prairie country.

We usually had early morning Christmas with the Merwins at Grandfather Davis', before we went on for the second half of the double-header day: more presents and another tree, at Grandfather Stevenson's. One of my most thrilling presents was a doll's brass bed with pillows, sheets and blankets, from Aunt Letitia. Another was the silver comb, brush and mirror Grandmother gave me, piece by piece, engraved with a rose and my name, Elizabeth. Adlai's favorite was his toy train, which he kept set up in the attic, where he could crash his cars in harrowing imitation of the wrecks that were all too frequent in that day.

One year our pre-Christmas curiosity reached such a pitch we sneaked into the guestroom when our parents were out, crawled up on the closet shelf, and examined every one of the presents Mother and Father had carefully hidden away. Then our guilty consciences made us exclaim all the louder on Christmas morning, over "surprises" that included a tool chest for Adlai, and for me a doll's purple velvet coat and matching hat with plumes that Mother had made.

Whenever our Hardin cousins came for the holidays, they livened things up considerably. Our handsome Aunt Julia, father's sister, was married to a Presbyterian minister, Reverend Martin Hardin II, and they had a daughter Letitia and three rambunctious sons. There was a great uproar the time young Letitia was missing all day, and by late afternoon the frantic grownups called the police, to help search. Eventually they found our cousin sitting peacefully upstairs in Grandfather's attic, surrounded by three thousand books, reading her way through them as a mouse nibbles through cheese.

Her brothers were active in a less literary way, and Adlai went right along. Once at dinner the boys snapped butter balls up at the ceiling, and a few stuck there and quivered suspensefully over the chatting grownups' oblivious heads. They also staged shooting frays with Concord grapes—one strategic squeeze and the grape's innards would squirt out and plop juicily on the target.

For more conventional amusement at holiday parties we played charades. Once Adlai lay down on the floor, curled up in a ball, and stymied all guests. It turned out he was a "sunbeam on a rug." Then I came leaping in waving my arms wildly; this was intended to depict "the soaring of a soul."

Memories, Dreams, and the Poor
by Floyd Dell

Memories of childhood are strange things. The obscurity of the past opens upon a little lighted space—a scene, unconnected with anything else. One must figure out when it happened. There may be anomalies in the scene, which need explanation. Sometimes the scenes are tiny fragments only. Again they are long dramas. Having once been remembered, they can be lived through again in every moment, with a detailed experiencing of movement and sensation and thought. One can start the scene in one's mind and see it all through again. Exactly so it was—clearer in memory than something that happened yesterday, though it was forty years ago. And, oddly enough, if there is some detail skipped over, lost out of the memory picture, no repetition of the remembering process will supply it—the gap is always there.

That fall, before it was discovered that the soles of both my shoes were worn clear through, I still went to Sunday school. And one time the Sunday-school superintendent made a speech to all the classes. He said that these were hard times, and that many poor children weren't getting enough to eat. It was the first that I had heard about it. He asked everybody to bring some food for the poor children next Sunday. I felt very sorry for the poor children.

Also, little envelopes were distributed to all the classes. Each little boy and girl was to bring money for the poor, next Sunday. The pretty Sunday-school teacher explained that we were to write our names, or have our parents write them, up in the left-hand corner of the little envelopes. . . . I told my mother all about it when I came home. And my mother gave me, the next Sunday, a small bag of potatoes to carry to Sunday school. I supposed the poor children's mothers would make potato soup out of them. . . . Potato soup was good. My father, who was quite a joker, would always say, as if he were surprised, "Ah! I see we have some nourishing potato soup today!" It was so good that we had it every day. My father was at home all day long and every day, now; and I liked that, even if he was grumpy as he sat reading Grant's 'Memoirs.' I had my parents all to myself, too; the others were away. My oldest brother was in Quincy, and memory does not reveal where the others were: perhaps with relatives in the country.

Taking my small bag of potatoes to Sunday school, I looked around for the poor children; I was disappointed not to see them. I had heard about poor children in stories. But I was told just to put my contribution with the others on the big table in the side room.

I had brought with me the little yellow envelope, with some money in it for the poor children. My mother had put the money in it and sealed it up. She wouldn't tell me how much money she had put in it, but it felt like several dimes. Only she wouldn't let me write my name on the envelope. I had learned to write my name, and I was proud of being able to do it. But my mother said firmly, *no*, I must *not* write my name on the envelope; she didn't tell me why. On the way to Sunday school I had pressed the envelope against the coins until I could tell what they were; they weren't dimes but pennies.

When I handed in my envelope, my Sunday-school teacher noticed that my name wasn't on it, and she gave me a pencil; I could write my own name, she said. So I did. But I was confused because my mother had said not to; and when I came home, I confessed what I had done. She looked distressed. "I told you not to!" she said. But she didn't explain why. . . .

I didn't go back to school that fall. My mother said it was because I was sick. I did have a cold the week that school opened; I had been playing in the gutters and had got my feet wet, because there were holes in my shoes. My father cut insoles out of cardboard, and I wore those in my shoes. As long as I had to stay in the house anyway, they were all right.

I stayed cooped up in the house, without any companionship. We didn't take a Sunday paper any more, but the Barry Adage came every week in the mails; and though I did not read small print, I could see the Santa Clauses and holly wreaths in the advertisements.

There was a calendar in the kitchen. The red days were Sundays and holidays; and that red 25 was Christmas. (It was on a Monday, and the two red figures would come right together in 1893; but this represents research in the World Almanac, not memory.) I knew when Sunday was, because I could look out of the window and see the neighbor's children, all dressed up, going to Sunday school. I knew just when Christmas was going to be.

But there was something queer! My father and mother didn't say a word about Christmas. And once, when I spoke of it, there was a strange, embarrassed silence; so I didn't say anything more about it. But I wondered, and was troubled. Why didn't they say anything about it? Was what I had said I wanted (memory refuses to supply that detail) too expensive?

I wasn't arrogant and talkative now. I was silent and frightened. What was the matter? Why didn't my father and mother say anything about Christmas? As the day approached, my chest grew tighter with anxiety.

Now it was the day before Christmas. I couldn't be mistaken. But not a word about it from my father and mother. I waited in painful bewilderment all day. I had supper with them, and was allowed to sit up for an hour. I was waiting for them to say something. "It's time for you to go to bed," my mother said gently. I *had* to say something.

"This is Christmas Eve, isn't it?" I asked, as if I didn't know.

My father and mother looked at one another. Then my mother looked away. Her face was pale and stony. My father cleared his throat, and his face took on a joking look. He pretended he hadn't known it was Christmas Eve, because he hadn't been reading the papers. He said he would go downtown and find out.

My mother got up and walked out of the room. I didn't want my father to have to keep on being funny about it, so I got up and went to bed. I went by myself without having a light. I undressed in the dark and crawled into bed.

I was numb. As if I had been hit by something. It was hard to breathe. I ached all through. I was stunned—with finding out the truth.

My body knew before my mind quite did. In a minute, when I could think, my mind would know. And as the pain in my body ebbed, the pain in my mind began. I *knew*. I couldn't put it into words yet. But I knew why I had taken only a little bag of potatoes to Sunday school that fall. I knew why there had been only pennies in my little yellow envelope. I knew why I hadn't gone to school that fall—why I hadn't any new shoes—why we had been living on potato soup all winter. All these things, and others, many others, fitted themselves together in my mind, and meant something.

Then the words came into my mind and I whispered them into the darkness:

"*We're poor!*"

That was it. I was one of those poor children I had been sorry for, when I heard about them in Sunday school. My mother hadn't told me. My father was out of work, and we hadn't any money. That was why there wasn't going to be any Christmas at our house.

Then I remembered something that made me squirm with shame—a boast. (Memory will not yield this up. Had I said to some Nice little boy, "I'm going to be President of the United States"? Or to a Nice little girl: "I'll marry you when I grow up"? It was some boast as horribly shameful to remember.)

"*We're poor.*" There in bed in the dark, I whispered it over and over to myself. I was making myself get used to it. (Or—just torturing myself, as one presses the tongue against a sore tooth? No, memory says not like that—but to keep myself from ever being such a fool again: suffering now, to keep this awful thing from ever happening again. Memory is clear on that; it was more like pulling the tooth, to get it over with—never mind the pain, this will be the end!)

It wasn't so bad, now that I knew. I just *hadn't known*! I had thought all sorts of foolish things: that I was going to Ann Arbor—going to be a lawyer—going to make speeches in the Square, going to be President. Now I knew better.

I had wanted (something) for Christmas. I didn't want it, now.

I didn't want anything.

I lay there in the dark, feeling the cold emotion of renunciation. (The tendrils of desire unfold their clasp on the outer world of objects, withdraw, shrivel up. Wishes shrivel up, turn black, die. It is like that.)

It hurt. But nothing would ever hurt again. I would never let myself want anything again.

I lay there stretched out straight and stiff in the dark, my fists clenched hard upon Nothing. . . .

In the morning it had been like a nightmare that is not clearly remembered—that one wishes to forget. Though I hadn't hung up any stocking, there was one hanging at the foot of my bed. A bag of popcorn, and a lead pencil, for me. They had done the best they could, now they realized that I knew about Christmas. But they needn't have thought they had to. I didn't want anything.

Literary critic, editor, novelist, and Broadway playwright Floyd Dell was born in Pike County at Barry in 1887, and lived in several Mississippi river-towns during his youth.

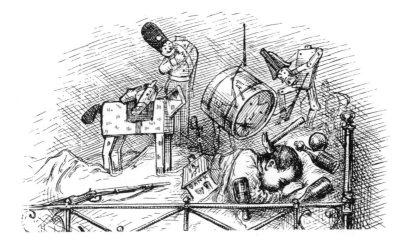

Peoria to Chicago

by Mrs. Everett M. Dirksen

Ours was a small wedding. We had neither very much money nor family. I had only my mother and Everett had only his two brothers.

We were married in my mother's house with a simple ceremony at 6 p.m. on Christmas Eve of 1927. A friend of mine from Peoria was my maid of honor and Everett's twin brother Tom was his best man.

The ceremony was followed by refreshments—my mother's homemade cake and ice cream.

We heard later that our next-door neighbors had peeked in the window and watched the wedding and thought it was lovely.

I wore a blue velvet wedding dress and a hat made of little silver discs that fitted over my head like a soup bowl. I was still working in the department store in Peoria, so I was able to purcase my dress with my employee discount. It cost $35 and was in the high-fashion style of those days with the waistline down around the hips and the skirt just a touch below the knee. (The Grace Coolidge type.)

Everett had given up his job with the dredging company, thank goodness, and only recently had gone into the bakery business with his two brothers. It was started on a shoestring and barely struggling along, so there was not much money for a honeymoon.

But one of the first things Everett had asked me when we were planning our wedding was whether I would like to spend our honeymoon in Chicago. Would I! I had never been to Chicago. But then, he needn't have asked. I would have gone anywhere with him, even on a sloppy dredge boat.

He had warned me ahead of time that we would have only three days for our honeymoon. That was all he could afford. He had to get back to the bakery.

So, as soon as the cake and ice cream were served at our wedding, we left for the railway station to take the midnight Rock Island train to Chicago. It was an overnight trip from Pekin, and we sat up all night in the coach. There was not enough money for both a berth *and* the honeymoon.

Our train chugged into Chicago at 7 a.m. on Christmas Day.

We stayed at the Morrison Hotel in the heart of the Loop. We could walk to almost any place downtown from there, and walk we did.

To the F. Scott Fitzgeralds

We combed the Avenue this last month
A hundred times if we combed it onth,
In search of something we thought would do
To give to a person as nice as you.

We had no trouble selecting gifts
For the Ogden Armours and Louie Swifts,
The Otto Kahns and the George E. Bakers,
The Munns and the Rodman Wanamakers.

It's a simple matter to pick things out
For people one isn't so wild about,
But you, you wonderful pal and friend, you!
We couldn't find anything fit to send you.

The Ring Lardners

The following Christmas they got this reply from the Fitzgeralds:

To the Ring Lardners

You combed the Avenue last year
For some small gift that was not too dear
—Like a candy cane or a worn out truss—
To give to a loving friend like us.
You'd found gold eggs for such wealthy hicks
As the Edsell (*sic*) Fords and the Pittsburgh Fricks,
The Andy Mellons, the Teddy Shonts,
The Coleman T. and Pierre duPonts,
But not one gift to brighten our hoem
—So I'm sending you back your God damn poem.

You Know Me Al

by Ring Lardner

Old Pal: I guess all these lefthanders is alike though I thought this Allen had some sense. I thought he was different from the most and was not no rummy but they are all alike Al and they are all lucky that somebody don't hit them over the head with a ax and kill them but I guess at that you could not hurt no lefthanders by hitting them over the head. We was all down on State St. the day before Xmas and the girls was all tired out and ready to go home but Allen says No I guess we better stick down a while because now the crowds is out and it will be fun to watch them. So we walked up and down State St. about a hour longer and finally we come in front of a big jewelry store window and in it was a swell diamond ring that was marked $100. It was a ladies' ring so Marie says to Allen Why don't you buy that for me? And Allen says Do you really want it? And she says she did.

So we tells the girls to wait and we goes over to a salloon where Allen has got a friend and gets a check cashed and we come back and he bought the ring. Then Florrie looks like as though she was getting all ready to cry and I asked her what was the matter and she says I had not boughten her no ring not even when we was engaged. So I and Allen goes back to the salloon and I gets a check cashed and we come back and bought another ring but I did not think the ring Allen had boughten was worth no $100 so I gets one for $75. Now Al you know I am not makeing no kick on spending a little money for a present for my own wife but I had allready boughten her a rist watch for $15 and a rist watch was just what she had wanted. I was willing to give her the ring if she had not of wanted the rist watch more than the ring but when I give her the ring I kept the rist watch and did not tell her nothing about it.

Well I come downtown alone the day after Xmas and they would not take the rist watch back in the store where I got it. So I am going to give it to her for a New Year's present and I guess that will make Allen feel like a dirty doose. But I guess you cannot hurt no lefthander's feelings at that. They are all alike. But Allen has not got nothing but a dinky curve ball and a fast ball that looks like my slow one. If Comiskey was not good hearted he would of sold him long ago.

I sent you and Bertha a cut glass dish Al which was the best I could get for the money and it was pretty high pricet at that. We was glad to get the pretty pincushions from you and Bertha and Florrie says to tell you that we are well supplied with pincushions now because the ones you sent makes a even half dozen. Thanks Al for remembering us and thank Bertha too though I guess you paid for them.

Your pal, Jack.

Ring Lardner wrote sport columns for Chicago newspapers, the Inter-Ocean, Examiner, *and* Tribune *after his break into big city journalism during the 1907 World Series. He also wrote humorous columns, short stories and plays for which he has received lasting fame.*

About Myself
by Theodore Dreiser

Wanted: A number of bright young men to assist in the business department during the Christmas holidays. Promotion possible. Apply to Business Manager between 9 and 10 a.m.

"Here," I thought as I read it, "is just the thing I am looking for. Here is this great paper, one of the most prosperous in Chicago, and here is an opening for me. If I can only get this my fortune is made. I shall rise rapidly." I conceived of myself as being sent off the same day, as it were, on some brilliant mission and returning, somehow, covered with glory.

I hurried to the office of the *Herald,* in Washington Street near Fifth Avenue, this same morning, and asked to see the business manager. After a short wait I was permitted to enter the sanctuary of this great person, who to me, because of the material splendor of the front office, seemed to be the equal of a millionaire at least. He was tall, graceful, dark, his full black whiskers parted aristocratically in the middle of his chin, his eyes vague pools of subtlety. "See what a wonderful thing it is to be connected with the newspaper business!" I told myself.

"I saw your ad in this morning's paper," I said hopefully.

"Yes, I did want a half dozen young men," he replied, beaming upon me reassuringly, "but I think I have nearly enough. Most of the young men that come here seem to think they are to be connected with the *Herald* direct, but the fact is we want them only for clerks in our free Christmas gift bureau. They have to judge whether or not the applicants are impostors and keep people from imposing on the paper. The work will only be for a week or ten days, but you will probably earn ten or twelve dollars in that time—" My heart sank. "After the first of the year, if you take it, you may come around to see me. I may have something for you."

When he spoke of the free Christmas gift bureau I vaguely understood what he meant. For weeks past, the *Herald* had been conducting a campaign for gifts for the poorest children of the city. It had been importuning the rich and the moderately comfortable to give, through the medium of its scheme, which was a bureau for the free distribution of all such things as could be gathered via cash or direct donation of supplies: toys, clothing, even food, for children.

"But I wanted to become a reporter if I could," I suggested.

"Well," he said, with a wave of his hand, "this is as good a way as any other. When this is over I may be able to introduce you to our city editor." The title, "city editor," mystified and intrigued me. It sounded so big and significant.

This offer was far from what I anticipated, but I took it joyfully. Thus to step from one job to another, however brief, and one with such prospects, seemed the greatest luck in the world.

I bustled about to the *Herald's* Christmas Annex, as it was called, a building standing in Fifth Avenue between Madison and Monroe, and reported to a brisk underling in charge of the doling out of these pittances to the poor. Without a word he put me behind the single long counter which ran across the front of the room and over which were handled all those toys and Christmas pleasure pieces which a loud tomtoming concerning the dire need of the poor and the proper Christmas spirit had produced.

Life certainly offers some amusing paradoxes at times, and that with that gay insouciance which life alone can muster and achieve when it is at its worst anachronistically. Here was I, a victim of what Socialists would look upon as wage slavery and economic robbery, quite as worthy, I am sure, of gifts as any other, and yet lined up with fifteen or twenty other economic victims, ragamuffin souls like myself, all out of jobs, many of them out at elbows, and all of them doling out gifts from eight-thirty in the morning until eleven and twelve at night to people no worse off than themselves.

I wish you might have seen this chamber as I saw it for eight or nine days just preceding and including Christmas day itself. (Yes; we worked from eight a.m. to five-thirty p.m. on Christmas day, and very glad to get the money, thank you.) There poured in here from the day the bureau opened, which was the morning I called, and until it closed Christmas night, as diverse an assortment of alleged poverty-stricken souls as one would want to see. I do not say that many of them were not deserving; I am willing to believe that most of them were; but, deserving or no, they were still worthy of all they received here. Indeed when I think of the many who came miles, carrying slips of paper on which had been listed, as per the advice of this paper, all they wished Santa Claus to bring them or their children, and then recall that, for all their pains in having their minister or doctor or the *Herald* itself visé their request, they received only a fraction of what they sought, I am inclined to think that all were even more deserving than their reward indicated.

For the whole scheme, as I soon found in talking with others and seeing for myself how it worked, was most loosely managed. Endless varieties of toys and comforts had been talked about in the paper, but only a few of the things promised, or vaguely indicated, were here to give—for the very good reason that no one would give them for nothing to the *Herald*. Nor had any sensible plan been devised for checking up either the gifts given or the person who had received them, and so the same person, as some of these recipients soon discovered, could come over and over, bearing different lists of toys, and get them, or at least a part of them, until some clerk with a better eye for faces than another would chance to recognize the offender and point him or her out. The *Herald* was supposed to have kept all applications written by children to Santa Claus, but it had not done so, and so hundreds claimed that they had written letters and received no answer. At the end of the second or third day before Christmas it was found necessary, because of the confusion and uncertainty, to throw the doors wide open and give to all and sundry who looked worthy of whatever was left or "handy," we, the ragamuffin clerks, being the judges.

And now the clerks themselves, seeing that no records were kept and how without plan the whole thing was, notified poor relatives and friends, and these descended upon us with baskets, expecting candy, turkeys, suits of clothing and the like, but receiving instead only toy wagons, toy stoves, baby brooms, Noah's Arks, story books—the shabbiest mess of cheap things one could imagine. For the newspaper, true to that canon of commerce which demands the most for the least, the greatest show for the least money, had gathered all the odds and ends and left-overs of toy bargain sales and had dumped them into the large lofts above, to be doled out as best we could. We could not give a much-desired article to any one person because, supposing it were there, which was rarely the case, we could not get at it or find it; yet later another person might apply and receive the very thing the other had wanted.

And we clerks, going out to lunch or dinner (save the mark!), would seek some scrubby little restaurant and eat ham and beans, or crullers and coffee, or some other tasteless dish, at ten or fifteen cents per head. Hard luck stories, comments on what a botch the *Herald* gift bureau was, on the strange characters that showed up were the order of the day. Here I met a young newspaper man, gloomy, out at elbows, who told me what a wretched, pathetic struggle the newspaper world presented, but I did not believe him although he had worked in Chicago, Denver, St. Paul.

"A poor failure," I thought, "some one who can't write and who now whines and wastes his substance in riotous living when he has it!"

So much for the sympathy of the poor for the poor.

But the *Herald* was doing very well. Daily it was filling its pages with the splendid results of its charity, the poor relieved, the darkling homes restored to gayety and bliss. . . . Can you beat it? But it was good advertising, and that was all the *Herald* wanted.

Hey, Rub-a-dub! Hey, Rub-a-dub-dub!

Though born (1871) and raised in small towns, Theodore Dreiser and his family were drawn repeatedly to Chicago where he began his writing career and developed into one of the "realists" of the Chicago school. His best known works are Sister Carrie *and* An American Tragedy.

One Christmas Eve

by Langston Hughes

Standing over the hot stove cooking supper, the colored maid, Arcie, was very tired. Between meals today, she had cleaned the whole house for the white family she worked for, getting ready for Christmas tomorrow. Now her back ached and her head felt faint from sheer fatigue. Well, she would be off in a little while, if only the Missus and her children would come on home to dinner. They were out shopping for more things for the tree which stood all ready, tinsel-hung and lovely in the living-room, waiting for its candles to be lighted.

Arcie wished she could afford a tree for Joe. He'd never had one yet, and it's nice to have such things when you're little. Joe was five, going on six. Arcie, looking at the roast in the white folks' oven, wondered how much she could afford to spend tonight on toys. She only got seven dollars a week, and four of that went for her room and the landlady's daily looking after Joe while Arcie was at work.

"Lord, it's more'n a notion raisin' a child," she thought.

She looked at the clock on the kitchen table. After seven. What made white folks so darned inconsiderate? Why didn't they come on home here to supper? They knew she wanted to get off before all the stores closed. She wouldn't have time to buy Joe nothin' if they didn't hurry. And her landlady probably wanting to go out and shop, too, and not be bothered with little Joe.

"Dog gone it!" Arcie said to herself. "If I just had my money, I might leave the supper on the stove for 'em. I just got to get to the stores fo' they close." But she hadn't been paid for the week yet. The Missus had promised to pay her Christmas Eve, a day or so ahead of time.

Arcie heard a door slam and talking and laughter in the front of the house. She went in and saw the Missus and her kids shaking snow off their coats.

"Umm-mm! It's swell for Christmas Eve," one of the kids said to Arcie. "It's snowin' like the deuce, and mother came near driving through a stop light. Can't hardly see for the snow. It's swell!"

"Supper's ready," Arcie said. She was thinking how her shoes weren't very good for walking in snow.

It seemed like the white folks took as long as they could to eat that evening. While Arcie was washing dishes, the Missus came out with her money.

"Arcie," the Missus said, "I'm so sorry, but would you mind if I just gave you five dollars tonight? The children have made me run short of change, buying presents and all."

"I'd like to have seven," Arcie said. "I needs it."

"Well, I just haven't got seven," the Missus said. "I didn't know you'd want all your money before the end of the week, anyhow. I just haven't got it to spare."

Arcie took five. Coming out of the hot kitchen, she wrapped up as well as she could and hurried by the house where she roomed to get little Joe. At least he could look at the Christmas trees in the windows downtown.

The landlady, a big light yellow woman, was in a bad humor. She said to Arcie, "I thought you was comin' home early and get this child. I guess you know I want to go out, too, once in awhile."

Arcie didn't say anything for, if she had, she knew the landlady would probably throw it up to her that she wasn't getting paid to look after a child both night and day.

"Come on, Joe," Arcie said to her son, "let's us go in the street."

"I hears they got a Santa Claus down town," Joe said, wriggling into his worn little coat. "I wants to see him."

"Don't know 'bout that," his mother said, "but hurry up and get your rubbers on. Stores'll all be closed directly."

It was six or eight blocks downtown. They trudged along through the falling snow, both of them a little cold. But the snow was pretty!

The main street was hung with bright red and blue lights. In front of the City Hall there was a Christmas tree—but it didn't have no presents on it, only lights. In the store windows there were lots of toys—for sale.

Joe kept on saying, "Mama, I want . . ."

But mama kept walking ahead. It was nearly ten, when the stores were due to close, and Arcie wanted to get Joe some cheap gloves and something to keep him warm, as well as a toy or two. She thought she might come across a rummage sale where they had children's clothes. And in the ten-cent store, she could get some toys.

"O-oo! Lookee . . .," little Joe kept saying, and pointing at things in the windows. How warm and pretty the lights were, and the shops, and the electric signs through the snow.

It took Arcie more than a dollar to get Joe's mittens and things he needed. In the A. & P. Arcie bought a big box of hard candies for 49¢. And then she guided Joe through the crowd on the street until they came to the dime store. Near the ten-cent store they passed a moving picture theatre. Joe said he wanted to go in and see the movies.

Arcie said, "Ump-un! No, child! This ain't a city where they have shows for colored, too. In these here small towns, they don't let colored folks in. We can't go in there."

"Oh," said little Joe.

In the ten-cent store, there was an awful crowd. Arcie told Joe to stand outside and wait for her. Keeping hold of him in the crowded store would be a job. Besides she didn't want him to see what toys she was buying. They were to be a surprise from Santa Claus tomorrow.

Little Joe stood outside the ten-cent store in the light, and the snow, and people passing. Gee, Christmas was pretty. All tinsel and stars and cotton. And Santa Claus a-coming from somewhere, dropping things in stockings. And all the people in the streets were carrying things, and the kids looked happy.

But Joe soon got tired of just standing and thinking and waiting in front of the ten-cent store. There were so many things to look at in the other windows. He moved along up the block a little, and then a little more, walking and looking. In fact, he moved until he came to the white folks' picture show.

In the lobby of the moving picture show, behind the plate glass doors, it was all warm and glowing and awful pretty. Joe stood looking in, and as he looked his eyes began to make out, in there blazing beneath holly and colored streamers and the electric stars of the lobby, a marvellous Christmas tree. A group of children and grown-ups, white, of course, were standing around a big jovial man in red beside the tree. Or was it a man? Little Joe's eyes opened wide. No, it was not a man at all. It was Santa Claus!

Little Joe pushed open one of the glass doors and ran into the lobby of the white moving picture show. Little Joe went right through the crowd and up to where he could get a good look at Santa Claus. And Santa Claus was giving away gifts, little presents for children, little boxes of animal crackers and stick-candy canes. And behind him on the tree was a big sign (which little Joe didn't know how to read). It said, to those who understood, MERRY XMAS FROM SANTA CLAUS TO OUR YOUNG PATRONS.

Around the lobby, other signs said, WHEN YOU COME OUT OF THE SHOW STOP WITH YOUR CHILDREN AND SEE OUR SANTA CLAUS. And another announced, GEM THEATRE MAKES ITS CUSTOMERS HAPPY—SEE OUR SANTA.

And there was Santa Claus in a red suit and a white beard all sprinkled with tinsel snow. Around him were rattles and drums and rocking horses which he was not giving away. But the signs on them said (could little Joe have read) that they would be presented from the stage on Christmas Day to the holders of the lucky numbers. Tonight, Santa Claus was only giving away candy, and stick-candy canes, and animal crackers to the kids.

Joe would have liked terribly to have a stick-candy cane. He came a little closer to Santa Claus, until he was right in the front of the crowd. And then Santa Claus saw Joe.

Why is it that lots of white people always grin when they see a Negro child? Santa Claus grinned. Everybody else grinned, too, looking at little black Joe—who had no business in the lobby of a white theatre. Then Santa Claus stooped down and slyly picked up one of his lucky number rattles, a great big loud tin-pan rattle such as they use in cabarets. And he shook it fiercely right at Joe. That was funny. The white people laughed, kids and all. But little Joe didn't laugh. He was scared. To the shaking of the big rattle, he turned and fled out of the warm lobby of the theatre, out into the street where the snow was and the people. Frightened by laughter, he had begun to cry. He went looking for his mama. In his heart he never thought Santa Claus shook great rattles at children like that —and then laughed.

In the crowd on the street he went the wrong way. He couldn't find the ten-cent store or his mother. There were too many people, all white people, moving like white shadows in the snow, a world of white people.

It seemed to Joe an awfully long time till he suddenly saw Arcie, dark and worried-looking, cut across the side-walk through the passing crowd and grab him. Although her arms were full of packages, she still managed with one free hand to shake him until his teeth rattled.

"Why didn't you stand where I left you?" Arcie demanded loudly. "Tired as I am, I got to run all over the streets in the night lookin' for you. I'm a great mind to wear you out."

When little Joe got his breath back, on the way home, he told his mama he had been in the moving picture show.

"But Santa Claus didn't give me nothin'," Joe said tearfully. "He made a big noise at me and I runned out."

"Serves you right," said Arcie, trudging through the snow. "You had no business in there. I told you to stay where I left you."

"But I seed Santa Claus in there," little Joe said, "so I went in."

"Huh! That wasn't no Santa Claus," Arcie explained. "If it was, he wouldn't a treated you like that. That's a theatre for white folks—I told you once—and he's just a old white man."

"Oh . . . ," said little Joe.

Born in Joplin, Missouri, Langston Hughes was a well known poet and writer who as a young man lived in Chicago and there founded a black theater company.

God Rest Ye Merry
by MacKinlay Kantor

My child, you will see many strange things. . . . You will watch the holly berries wither and freeze while the nettles are pressed tenderly. . . . The good deer will starve in icy thickets when the rat grows portly amid his corn. . . . You will see the inspired creator neglected and his smug imitators extolled. . . . Hero ignored and presumptuous coward feted richly; these you will observe. . . . The shyster shall dwell long in luxury; the diligent and dependable will fall early, and on the dole. . . . A kindly nation may shiver in terror of the iron harshness adopted by its neighbors. . . . Bright universe eclipsed, black tarn gilded by a permanent sun: you see your future so. . . . And yet in their season the candles will be lighted again, the cones smell pungent; men may sing with the tongues and throats of angels amid the saintliest frost. . . . There is time now for consideration of the noblest Tale of all, if one be willing to cry again, and believe: 'God Rest Ye Merry—' in the midnight clear.

MacKinley Kantor came to Chicago to make his way in a writing career and found a wife as well, as he relates in his autobiographical I Love You, Irene. *He won a Pulitzer Prize for* Andersonville.

Ole Saint (Hic!)
by Mike Royko

The woman was very upset. She had taken her small son to see Santa Claus at a department store in one of the nearby, blue-collar suburbs. The boy had waited his turn in line, climbed on Santa's knee and had gone through the ritual of saying he had been good and describing the gifts he wanted.

The boy's mother had stood nearby. Close enough, she said, so that she could sniff the air and notice the definite odor of whiskey.

"The man was half stewed," she said. "I got close enough to get a look at his eyes. They were glassy and he reeked of liquor. His speech was kind of slurred and his face was flushed. Very red.

"When my boy finished, I asked the man if he had been drinking. I told him that I didn't think he should expose children to that kind of thing. He said: "Don't worry, lady, I haven't dropped a kid yet."

"So I went to the manager of the store and told him that I thought he had a drunken Santa Claus. He just shrugged and said that they hadn't had any other complaints about him and that he was the best Santa Claus they could find.

"My son heard all this, and in the car on the way home, he asked me: 'Mom, was Santa drunk?' I didn't know what to tell him. How do you explain something like that to an impressionable child."

The woman then suggested that I call the manager of the store and chide him for exposing children to a half-stewed Santa Claus.

But I can't bring myself to do it.

For one thing, there is something of a tradition in department store Santas being a bit juiced.

The first Santa I ever saw was in a store in Milwaukee and Division. As I was in the middle of telling him about the sled and pirate pistols I wanted, his eyes rolled up in his head and he appeared to pass out.

My mother, an understanding and quick-thinking woman said: "It is a long ride from the North Pole to Chicago. He must be very tired."

Slats Grobnik, who was next in line, said: "Yeah, my fodder gets tired like that every Friday and Saturday night, and at weddings, too."

Jon Hahn, a former Chicago newspaperman, once told me about a traumatic experience he had with a neighborhood department store Santa.

"We went to see him on Christmas Eve, in the afternoon," Hahn recalled. "I thought something was kind of strange about him because his leg kept collapsing and the kids would slide off onto the floor.

"Then later, when we got home, my mother told me to run down to the corner tavern and tell my father to come home for dinner before he spent his Christmas bonus.

"When I walked into the tavern, there was my father and Santa Claus—the one from that department store—in the middle of the barroom throwing punches at each other.

"I don't remember what caused the argument, but I'll bet not many kids ever saw their father and Santa Claus duking it out on Christmas Eve."

There are probably reasons for the tendency among some store Santas to be drinking men.

It might have something to do with being exposed to so many children. Any school teacher can tell you what being in the same room with thirty or forty little kids all day can do to your stomach lining. And if you've ever had to run a birthday party for a couple of dozen of them, you know what a terrible experience that can be.

So I would think that the experience of sitting for hours, with dozens and dozens of the little buggers, climbing on your knee, would be enough to frazzle the nerves.

Even worse is the whole atmosphere of deceit, lying, greed, and materialism that permeates the ritual.

Tradition requires that the Santa ask the child if he or she has been good all year.

They always say, yes, of course they've been good, which is usually an outright lie. The kid knows it and the store Santa knows it. Most kids are not good. They are nasty little creatures who try to make life miserable for adults and one another.

Then, after the kids lie about their behavior, the store Santa has to ask them what they want in their stockings. And they make their greedy, outrageous demands. I want this, I want that, bring me this and bring me that.

He, in turn, has to lie right back and say he will bring them just about everything they ask for. If you think about it, no politician—not even an alderman—has to tell as many lies about what promises he can deliver on.

And then they have to top it off with a jolly ho-ho. During the Christmas season, in a busy store, some of these guys probably have to say ho-ho 5,000 times. What a way to make a buck, saying ho-ho to thousands of kids with runny noses.

So I think that suburban woman, and everybody else, should be tolerant of an occasional bleary-eyed Santa. After all, nobody ever asks him what *he* wants in his stocking. And if he wants it with an olive or a lemon twist.

Mike Royko has been a columnist for a succession of Chicago papers, the Daily News, Sun Times, *and* Tribune. *Winner of a number of awards including the Pulitzer prize his columns have won him a national audience.*

Tradition and Maud Martha
by Gwendolyn Brooks

What she had wanted was a solid. She wanted shimmering form; warm, but hard as stone and as difficult to break. She had wanted to found—tradition. She had wanted to shape, for their use, for hers, for his, for little Paulette's, a set of falterless customs. She had wanted stone: here she was being wife to *him*, salving him, in every way considering and replenishing him—in short, here she was celebrating Christmas night by passing pretzels and beer.

He had done his part, was his claim. He had, had he not? lugged in a Christmas tree. So he had waited till early Christmas morning, when a tree was cheap; so he could not get the lights to burn; so the tinsel was insufficient and the gold balls few. He had promised a tree and he had gotten a tree, and that should be enough for everybody. Furthermore, Paulette had her blocks, her picture book, her doll buggy and her doll. So the doll's left elbow was chipped: more than that would be chipped before Paulette was through! And if the doll buggy was not like the Gold Coast buggies, that was too bad; that was too, too bad for Maud Martha, for Paulette. Here he was, whipping himself to death daily, that Maud Martha's stomach and Paulette's stomach might receive bread and milk and navy beans with tomato catsup, and he was taken to task because he had not furnished, in addition, a velvet-lined buggy with white-walled wheels! Oh yes that was what Maud Martha wanted, for her precious princess daughter, and no use denying. But she could just get out and work, that was all. She could just get out and grab herself a job and buy some of these beans and buggies. And in the meantime, she could just help entertain his friends. She was his wife, and he was the head of the family, and on Christmas night the least he could do, by God, and would do, by God, was stand his friends a good mug of beer. And to heck with, in fact, to hell with, her fruitcakes and coffees. Put Paulette to bed.

At Home, the buying of the Christmas tree was a ritual. Always it had come into the Brown household four days before Christmas, tall, but not too tall, and not too wide. Tinsel, bulbs, little Santa Clauses and snowmen, and the pretty gold and silver and colored balls did not have to be renewed oftener than once in five years because after Christmas they were always put securely away, on a special shelf in the basement, where they rested for a year. Black walnut candy, in little flat white sheets, crunchy, accompanied the tree, but it was never eaten until Christmas eve. Then, late at night, a family decorating party was held, Maud Martha, Helen and Harry giggling and teasing and occasionally handing up a ball or Santa Claus, while their father smiled benignly over all and strung and fitted and tinseled, and their mother brought in the black walnut candy and steaming cups of cocoa with whipped cream, and plain shortbread. And everything peaceful, sweet!

And there were the other customs. Easter customs. In childhood, never till Easter morning was "the change" made, the change from winter to spring underwear. Then, no matter how cold it happened to be, off came the heavy trappings and out, for Helen and Maud Martha, were set the new little patent leather shoes and white socks, the little b.v.d.'s and light petticoats, and for Harry, the new brown oxfords, and white shorts and sleeveless undershirts. The Easter eggs had always been dyed the night before, and in the morning, before Sunday school, the Easter baskets, full of chocolate eggs and candy bunnies and cotton bunnies, were handed round, but not eaten from until after Sunday school, and even then not much!—because there was more candy coming, and dyed eggs, too, to be received (and eaten on the spot) at the Sunday School Children's Easter Program, on which every one of them recited until Maud Martha was twelve.

What of October customs?—of pumpkins yellowly burning; of polished apples in a water-green bowl; of sheets for ghost costumes, surrendered up by Mama with a sigh?

And birthdays, with their pink and white cakes and candles, strawberry ice cream, and presents wrapped up carefully and tied with wide ribbons: whereas here was this man, who never considered giving his own mother a birthday bouquet, and dropped in his wife's lap a birthday box of drugstore candy (when he thought of it) wrapped in the drugstore green.

The dinner table, at home, was spread with a white white cloth, cheap but white and very white, and whatever was their best in china sat in cheerful dignity, firmly arranged, upon it. This man was not a lover of tablecloths, he could eat from a splintery board, he could eat from the earth.

She passed round Blatz, and inhaled the smoke of the guests' cigarettes, and watched the soaked tissue that had enfolded the corner Chicken Inn's burned barbecue drift listlessly to her rug. She removed from her waist the arm of Chuno Jones, Paul's best friend.

Chicagoan Gwendolyn Brooks, born in 1917, was the first black poet to win the Pulitzer Prize, for her semiautobiographical Annie Allen (1949), *and has since published many collections of prose and poetry.*

Celebrating
the Feast

During our stay at the mouth of the river, Pierre and Jacques killed three buffalo and four deer, one of which ran some distance with its heart split in two. We contented ourselves with killing three or four turkeys, out of the many that came around our lodging because they were almost dying of hunger. Jacques also brought in a partridge.

Jacques Marquette, December 12, 1674

An ailing Marquette ate well on that particular December day in what otherwise was a bleak winter. He spent his last Christmas in a cabin on the banks of the Chicago river within the boundaries of the modern day city of Chicago.

Fête de l'Année

The last of December, 1679, on the banks of the river, we killed only a buffalo and some wild turkeys, because the Indians had set fire to the dry grass of the prairies along our route. The deer had fled; and in spite of the effort made to find game, we subsisted merely through the providence of God, who grants aid at one time that he withholds at another. By the greatest good fortune in the world, when we had nothing more to eat we found a huge buffalo mired at the river's edge. It was so big that twelve of our men using a cable had difficulty in drawing it onto firm ground.

The first day of the year 1680 I made an exhortation after mass, wishing a happy new year to Sieur de la Salle and all his men; and after an earnest talk I entreated our discontented ones to gird themselves with patience, pointing out to them that God would provide for their wants, if we lived in harmony he would create means to sustain us.

Louis Hennepin

The gathering described by Hennepin took place at the site of a temporarily vacated Illinois Indian village on the Illinois river near the present day town of Utica. Four days later the French met the Illinois south of Lake Peoria and a grand winter celebration followed.

After spending the day rejoicing, dancing, and feasting, we assembled the chiefs of the villages on either side of the river. We let them know through our interpreter that we Franciscans had not come to them to gather beavers, but to bring them knowledge of the great Master of Life and to instruct their children. We told them that we had left our country beyond the sea (or, as the Indians call it, the great lake) to come live with them and be their good friends. We heard a succession of loud voices saying "Tepatoui Nicka," which means "That is a good thing to do, my brother; you did well to have such a thought."

Louis Hennepin, 1680

The Mythic Illinois

The French held the Illinois Indians in high esteem. Reports sent home by early missionaries and explorers undoubtedly influenced such thinkers as Jean Jacques Rousseau and writings on the "innate goodness" of man. The Illinois were a peace loving nation, living in large villages and cultivating corn, interestingly enough, in about the same area where it is grown today. Pumpkins, wild turkeys, cranberries, and maple syrup along with cornmeal and many other items comprised their diet.

Le Réveillon

French settlements in Illinois in the 18th century prospered; they were centered mainly in Kaskaskia and Cahokia along the Mississippi. The French were great lovers of feasts; Christmastide was the gayest season of their year. Midnight Mass on December 24, ended the Advent fast and the Fête de Noël commenced with le Réveillon, an enormous Christmas breakfast for family and friends. More church services and parties followed through the New Year until the Twelfth Night Ball on the eve of Epiphany, January 6.

While the old Réveillon was held in the middle of the night in many present day Illinois homes it is celebrated as a grand breakfast on Christmas Day. This bill of fare suggests not only the French tradition but also honors other ethnic groups which make up the Illinois Christmas heritage.

Le Réveillon Menu

Hot Spiced Apple Cider   Eggnog with Brandy
Swedish Potato Sausage   Baked Eggs
French Onion Cassarole   Corn Bread with Maple Syrup
Kaffee Kuchen (see page 22)

French Onion Casserole

8 medium onions, sliced 1/2" thick
2 slices bacon
1 c. green pepper, chopped
1 clove garlic, minced
1 - 8 oz. can tomato sauce
1/2 c. cooked ham, julienned
1/4 tsp. salt, dash pepper (optional)
1/2 c. cheddar cheeze, shredded

Cook sliced onion in boiling, salted water until tender, about 10 minutes. Drain well. Place in 1-1/2 quart casserole. In skillet fry bacon until crisp, add green pepper and garlic; sauté until tender. Drain excess fat. Stir in tomato sauce, ham, salt and pepper. Pour mixture over onions. Bake at 350° for 20 minutes. Sprinkle top with cheeze and return to oven until cheeze melts. Makes 8 servings.

Baked Eggs

1 Tbsp. flour	1 tsp. Worcestershire sauce
4 oz. sharp cheddar cheese, shredded	Or 1 Tbsp. horseradish sauce
8 oz. Swiss cheeze, shredded	1/2 c. milk
	6 eggs

In a medium bowl toss Swiss cheeze and flour. Place in ungreased 1-1/2 quart shallow round baking dish. Evenly sprinkle with cheddar cheeze. In a medium bowl beat eggs, milk, and choice of horseradish sauce or Worcestershire until well blended. Pour over cheezes. At this point you may add 1 cup julienned slices of ham, if desired. Cover and refrigerate up to 24 hours. About 1-1/4 hours before serving uncover dish and let stand at room temperature for 30 minutes. Preheat oven to 350°. Bake 35-40 minutes or until eggs are set when dish is shaken. Makes 6 servings.

Potatis Korv
(Swedish Potato Sausage)

2-1/2 lbs. ground pork	1 tsp. pepper
1-1/2 lbs. ground beef	2 Tbsp. salt (or less)
6 medium raw potatoes	3/4 tsp. allspice
1 c. scalded milk or beef broth	2 tsp. ginger
1 large onion	1 lb. casings

Grind potatoes and mix with ground meat, add spices, salt and milk. Mix thoroughly. Cut casings in desired lengths, tie one end of casing and fill, using a sausage stuffer or a large-mouthed funnel. Do not fill them too tightly or they will burst during cooking. Tie other end. To prepare, bring water to a boil, add sausage and boil gently 30 minutes. Can also be baked in a casserole if casings are unavailable.

I come now to the most important article of this country's growth, I mean Indian corn, which with Americans is cultivated on a far more extensive scale than anything else. There are several sorts of Indian corn, and of different colors, namely white, red, yellow and mixed. The Americans live mostly on corn bread.

English visitor to Illinois, 1822

Corn Bread with Whole Wheat

1-1/2 c. flour
1/2 c. whole wheat flour
2 c. cornmeal
1/2 c. sugar
4 tsp. baking powder

1 tsp. salt
2 c. milk
1/2 c. vegetable oil
2 eggs, beaten (3 egg whites may be substituted)

Preheat oven to 400°. Grease 9" x 13" baking pan. Combine dry ingredients. Beat eggs in separate bowl, add milk and oil. Add liquid mixture to dry ingredients, mixing just until ingredients are moistened. Pour batter into prepared pan. Bake 20-25 minutes, until wooden pick inserted near center comes out clean. Serve warm, with butter and warmed maple syrup. Makes 12 servings.

Feast at Fort Dearborn

by Ruth De Young

Tonight—when carols are heard in cottage and mansion, when pines and firs take on their festive load of tinsel and holly, when curly heads wander into dreamland with fond anticipation of Santa Claus—there are Chicagoans who will retell the story of that first Christmas celebrated by hardy forbears in a fort of logs on a snow-bound prairie.

It was a bitter cold night in 1804, they will tell. For a week the snow had been falling. Save for the prints of a hungry pack of wolves a perfect blanket of white spread across the prairies. Black ice was in the river and the lake was frozen far as the eye could see.

Across the river to the north where pine and spruce broke the landscape, Ouilmette, the Frenchman whose cabin adjoined the Kinzies, dragged a tree over the ice with the aid of ropes. The day before Capt. Whistler, builder and commandant of Fort Dearborn, had ordered that a pine be cut to add to the good cheer indoors.

Merry shouts as Ouilmette drew nearer the fort. Then the glad greeting of soldiers and "coureurs de bois" returning with a buck, wild turkeys, a jack rabbit, and a raccoon slung across the back of their Indian pony.

This was Christmas eve. The booty once deposited in the stockade, there was the raising of the tree, lighting of the candles and carols—"Adeste Fideles," "Noël," "Joy to the World"—not unlike today.

Christmas morning dawned bright and clear. All was bustle and confusion for the holiday feast. At noon it was spread—venison pasty in the center, flanked by a whole roast pig at either end. Turkeys alternated with prairie chicken, rabbit, and raccoon round the sides.

Then the Christmas pudding, blazing with brandy, carried in by the cook of the fort, and set before Mrs. Whistler. It was a signal to the officers. With one accord they rose, and with milk punch served in silver goblets made by John Kinzle, drank a toast to Jefferson and Henry Dearborn, secretary of war, under whose orders the fort had been erected.

A pause and suddenly the cry, "Indians! Indians!" just as they were finishing the last. Hearts stood still. To arms, ordered Capt.

Whistler, and to the block houses.

From the west across the ice, tall, gaunt figures drew nearer, one by one. A sudden shriek like that of a partridge and Capt. Whistler breathed easily and answered with a friendly cry. It was Black Partridge and his braves from the land of the Illinois come up to the Forks on their annual hunting expedition. They had planned to surprise the fort with some peltries, but the eagle eye of the sentry was too penetrating.

Welcomed indoors, the fife and drum corps broke into a dance. Mrs. Whistler and John Kinzie [playing his fiddle meantime] led off with a reel. The commandant and Mrs. Kinzie followed with a caper and curtsy at the other end of the room.

Suddenly a war whoop from the Indians and they joined in a corn dance, brandishing their tomahawks and feather brushes in the air.

Darkness drew on, the music subsided, the candles were lighted, and the gifts distributed—beads for the Indians, tobacco and pies for the soldiers, gay ribbons from Montreal for the ladies, bows and arrows and Indian dolls for the children.

And so ended the first Christmas on Lake Michigan's shore. It is a story to be preserved, for year by year as generations grow farther and farther away, there are fewer among us to help piece the tale together.

Plum Pudding from the Fort

Plum pudding does not contain plums but dried currants, raisins, and apples. It is not cooked as we think of pudding, but steamed in a container, reaching a breadish consistency. Suet is used in place of another type of fat; its very gradual melting insures a delicate crumb.

2 c. finely chopped suet	3 c. sifted flour
2 c. seedless raisins	1 tsp. soda
1 c. chopped apple	1/2 tsp. salt
1 c. currants	2 Tbsp. cinnamon
1 c. light molasses	1/2 tsp. cloves
1 c. cold water	1/2 tsp. allspice

Mix the first six ingredients together and set aside. In a separate container combine the dry ingredients. Add this to the first mixture and mix well. Fill pudding molds or cans (like 1 lb. coffee cans) with tightly fitting lids, but only 2/3 full. Place molds on a trivet in a heavy kettle over, not sitting in, one inch simmering water. Cover tightly and steam for three hours. Add additional water to steaming kettle as needed so water doesn't boil away. Remove from heat, remove lids, let stand a half hour, and unmold. Serve the pudding with a lemon hard sauce or the following wine sauce.

1 c. sugar	1 well-beaten egg
1 c. butter	1/2 c. brandy
1/2 c. red wine	

Cream together sugar and butter. Add the well beaten eggs and wine. Stir over, not in, boiling water several minutes until mixture is well heated. Flame the pudding with the 1/2 c. brandy as it is brought to the table. Note: Alcohol is released from wine and brandy with heat and is not a factor in the final product.

Game of all kinds was plentiful, from venison to quail. A Christmas dinner would not have been complete without a wild turkey at one end of the table and a baked ham at the other, followed by a blazing plum pudding later. There were wonderful trifles, charlotte russes, floating islands and sparkling calf's foot jelly. Their fruit in winter must be preserved in summer in heavy syrup or brandy.

Alice Snyder, *Galena Looking Back,* the 1840's

The lover of good food regards complacently the long rows of well dressed turkeys, which our country friends, mindful of the wants of the season, are pouring into market—said birds looking all the while as if they could scarcely contain their gravy in their impatience to be cooked for somebody's Christmas dinner.

Ottawa Free Trader, December 24, 1847

We noticed a whole wagon load of dressed turkeys on the streets yesterday and the owner was retailing them from his wagon. Sundry of our staid old citizens might be seen skedadling off with a fat turkey in their hands, which was doubtless intended to grace the Christmas dinner table.

Bloomington Pantagraph, December 24, 1862

The nights in winter are at once inexpressibly cold and poetically fine. The sky is almost invariably clear, and the stars shine with a brilliancy entirely unknown in the humid atmosphere of England. Cold as it was, often did I, during the first winter, stand at the door of our cabin, admiring their lustre.

Rebecca Burlend, 1837

Winter is Coming

The leaves have now fallen,
    The winds whistle by;
The birds are all leaving
    For winter is nigh.

The snow-flakes are coming,
    The ground will be white,
Mother earth will be sleeping
    Through winter's bright night.

The stars brightly glist'ning
    Thro' the frosty nights;
Remind us of the coming
    Of winter's delights.

So when 'tis cold without,
    We'll make it warm within.
And when the snow frisks about,
    New hopes will then begin.

Rockford Journal, December 9, 1871

Slight falls of snow commence the middle of December. There is rarely snow enough to make sleighing in the beaten tracks. The greatest depth seldom exceeds five inches. Very few conventional sleighs are kept. But the farmers usually keep a coarse vehicle on which they slide their produce to market and their wood home. They are pleasant rides. A slight fall of snow on the long grass gives the sleigh an easy, flowing motion and you glide as gaily over the prairies as you would along the fenced ways of the East with a foot of snow beneath your polished runner. Away you go with nothing to restrain your motions, the wide domain is all unfenced; the frost has bridged the sloughs; and your excursion is bounded only by time and the capacity of your steed.

Eliza W. Farnham, Life in Prairie Land Circa 1822

The streets were alive and astir all day with sleighs and sleighing parties, and far into the night the sound of merry bells and cheerful voices rang on the cold clear air. How we envied them, in our sanctum, "the bells and the belles," the happy fellows who were sleighing last evening.

Chicago Tribune, December 24, 1859

Forty ladies and gentlemen and several cans of oysters started from this city at about six o'clock Friday evening for a sleigh ride out to the Tyler House. Two sleighs with four horses each and two with two horses were well packed with human freight, and the sleighing being good and weather pleasant nothing was wanting which could contribute to the happiness of the participants. At about eight o'clock the party arrived at Tyler's, and a few minutes later Ostrander brought out his "fiddle and bow" and a portion of the party were soon gliding the mazy dance. As none of the party had taken tea before leaving the city, the ringing of the supper bell which was heard at about eleven o'clock was not an unwelcome sound, and the party were by no means tardy in paying a practical compliment to the well spread table. At two o'clock all were on board and homeward bound.

The evening was the pleasantest of the winter so far and nothing occurred to mar the occasion.

Galena Weekly Gazette, December 26, 1865

Fresh in my memory is getting off the train in the middle of the snow at Christmas time to meet my aunt and uncle, who had a farm near Morrison, Illinois. We'd climb into the sleigh with hot bricks at our feet, buffalo robes over our legs, and drive off with bells jingling and the frosty wind slashing the blood into my cheeks until it seemed they would burst.

Ronald Reagan

Charles Alexander Jr., a driver for the John Engels grocery store experienced this noon what probably was the fastest sleigh ride he will care for this winter. The horse became frightened on the way up Main Street and tried its utmost to break all go as you please records but Charles showed his horsemanship and strength and held on to the reins until he had the frenzied animal under control.

Galena Daily Gazette, December 14, 1909

If you want to witness a sight that will delight you, go to the confectionery and bakery, near the post office, and see the Christmas goods, such as sugar toys of all descriptions, fancy candies in a thousand new and beautiful shapes, and cakes piled upon cakes. Among the latter we observed pound cake, fruit cake, nut cake, sponge cake, macaronni, and every manner of sweet cake, besides mammoth frosted beauties, as sweet and palatable as they are ornamental. Besides these there are here all sorts of fruits in season, and plenty of nuts. Here is the place to get your Christmas goods.

Ottawa Free Trader, December 20, 1873

You know Santa Claus belongs to all churches, and to all sects, and to all American heathens as well. I do not know anyone who objects to him.

Vachel Lindsay

Where Santa Shops

Our readers are no doubt making extensive preparations for Christmas and New Years. That good old soul, Santa Claus, whom all the children love so dearly, has already begun making his purchases of candy, nuts, etcetera, to make glad the hearts of the wee ones all over the land. We have watched with considerable interest the mysterious movements of this world-renowned philanthropist, and desire to whisper the results of our observation. He is so very sly however that little folks particularly are at a loss to know how and when he procures such vast quantities of sweetmeats and other nice things. But we saw him and—listen! He buys his candies and nuts at Lamont's, East Rockford.

Rockford Journal, December 16, 1871

Gathering Nuts
by Albert Britt

Hickory nuts deserve a chapter of their own. Their shells were hard to crack, and it was harder still to extract the kernel from the convoluted and involuted interior, but once out the meat had a flavor and a sweetness all its own, superior in my memory to the pecan of the South or the famed chestnut of the East. Compared with the hickory nut the English walnut of commerce is without character or distinction. The nuts of the black hickory must not be confused with those of the white hickory, poor cousin of the black. These were thin-shelled and bitter, pig nuts we called them, and only pigs and chipmunks ate them willingly. Squirrels turned up their noses at them if real nuts were to be had.

Time was when black hickory trees were dotted through the timber around us, with here and there a towering specimen of the "big" variety strayed up from the Mississippi bottoms. The big nuts were about the size of English walnuts, but not up to the level of the smaller kind.

There were other nut trees in our Illinois timber, black walnuts and butternuts for example. Black walnuts are definitely edible, although the flavor it too pronounced for delicate palates. The outer casing of the nut produces a dark brown dye, as the picker's fingers will testify, akin to the color that northern troops saw on Confederate uniforms, when they had time to look closely. There were two of these beautiful trees in our dooryard, as the squirrels of the neighborhood well knew. We had a few butternuts, the nuts easier to crack and with a milder flavor than the walnut. Of course there were hazel nuts, bushels of them; but those are from bushes, not trees. We rated hazel nuts rather low in our scale of desirability, although their resemblence to the English filbert gave them some sentimental title to consideration.

When the first frosts came was the time to gather the nuts from the ground, where they had fallen through the night, and shake down those that still clung to the branches. Old men who have known those late fall afternoons with a nip in the air in spite of the golden sunshine can feel again the cool wind blowing in spite of the years and miles between and hear the rustle of the dead leaves through which they searched for hickory nuts. We dried them in the sun to make sure of the final touch of ripeness and then stored them against the long winter evenings. The proper place for cracking them was on the edge of a flatiron held between the knees—never on the polished face of the iron if you valued your life. Tapped gently but firmly with a hammer they would sometimes break neatly into halves, but not often. However, small the fractions they were always good. Cracking hickory nuts or walnuts was no job for a young man in a hurry. Farm cooks sprinkled nuts through cake, and they were often in homemade candy. My own version of gastronomic luxury was hickory nuts and a ripe apple, Snow preferred, eaten together. If Olympus overlooked this delicate combination the high gods missed a bet. At least that was the way it seemed to me long ago.

Apple Walnut Cake

3 eggs
1 c. salad oil
1-3/4 c. sugar
1-1/2 c. white flour
1/2 c. whole wheat flour
1/2 tsp. salt
1/2 tsp. baking soda
1 tbsp. cinnamon
5 c. apples, chopped
3/4 c. walnuts, chopped

Cream together eggs, oil, and sugar. Mix dry ingredients together, then add to first mixture, blending well. Combine chopped apples and nuts, folding carefully into batter until just mixed. Bake in a greased 9 x 13 inch pan for one hour, at 350° or in a bundt pan for 50-55 minutes. Serve warm with whipped cream or top with vanilla ice cream.

Clockwork motorboats,
Boxes of children's shoes,
Hammers boys can use,
Blankets, shawls and wraps,
Scarfs and gloves and caps,
Wreaths and bright festoons,
Whistling balloons,

And Christmas candies fine,
All sent but as a sign
That love may still be found
In babes the world around.

Giraffes are down below,
Tin herds of buffalo,
Deers and bears and hens,
Wooden pigs and pens,
A sort of Noah's ark,
With beasties on a lark,
Woolly cats and dogs,
Rubber jumping frogs,
Elephants that caper
And dolls of colored paper.

We toys are silly things,
But we may conquer kings.
The world must play again
And pray and love again.
Peace and good will to men.

Vachel Lindsay

Springfield, Illinois

December 31, 1871

Dear Cousin Theo,

I thank you very much for the nice book you sent me for Christmas. I am going to read it. I had lots of things in my stocking, a sled, a box of paints, and some pictures to paint, some candy, a horse and cart, a Mother Goose book. I have been to see two Christmas trees this year, and they had a real Santa Claus and who do you think it was? Why it was Fred Haydem all the time.

Give a kiss to Grandmama and Aunt Nellie and Mamie for me and a kiss for you.

From,

Birdie Bailhache (six years old)

Books and a Flexible Flyer
by Erwin Thompson (Alton, Illinois)

My aunts told the story of their Christmases in their childhood. Oranges were a rare treat, one apiece was all they ever hoped for. A very small bag of candy sometimes came their way. Candy was almost as hard to come by as oranges. It was eaten sparingly, looked at, tasted, hidden to assure privacy. They said sometimes Annie (my mother) had some of hers left several months later. One storebought gift was the rule.

In my own childhood memories I think the biggest thrill as far as Christmas gifts were concerned was the year that I was seven. The sled was a "Flexible Flyer Number Two," and the first thing I did was to start at our back door and coast down the Little Bottom road to the railroad station at the foot of the hill which bore my Grandfather's name for half a century.

It was a very special sled, being a good two inches higher than any of the sleds owned by my playmates. This was a big advantage in deep snow. I often "broke trail," and the smaller sleds could follow after the first track was made. We often took our sleds to school with us in the later years when I went to Randolph. Coasting down our hill was sure a good start on that long cold two mile walk!

Years later, after I was grown, I gave the sled to Charlie Lock's youngsters who lived on the other side of the creek at Lock Haven. This was probably in 1935, and money was a mighty scarce article. There were no lavish Christmas presents in our neighborhood for anybody.

In 1948 I was working for the Union Electric Gas Department. The Locks were living on East Ninth, just west of Langdon. I was helping install a new gas line into their house, and saw the sled in their basement. It had evidently not been used for some years, as the children were all grown and had homes of their own.

I had children of my own by that time, and didn't have nearly as good a sled as that one. (Wartime sleds were pretty sorry affairs, flimsy things with wooden runners. They wouldn't go down hill unless you pushed them!) They gave the sled back to me and I still have it. Our grandchildren use it with appreciation.

So—fifty-four years of service from my Flexible Flyer! We have replaced a couple of wooden cross members and all of the deck-boards, but I'd still rather have "Old Flexie" than any new sled they've got in the hardware store.

Books were a part of our family tradition. My aunt's cousin, Mabel Olmstead, taught school in St. Louis. She had no close family left, so spent many weekends and holidays with us. The books she gave me were from Scribners or Doubleday, fine copies by such excellent artists as N. C. Wyth, The Swiss Family Robinson, The Boy Emigrant, Jinglebob, Lone Cowboy (Will James' autobiography, illustrated with his own drawings). These and many more were my treasured gifts, and a heritage I have passed along to my children, as well as the love and appreciation of good literature. They in turn have passed on the love and understanding, as well as the books themselves, to their own children. I still feel the magic of a good book.

Christmas in Grafton, Illinois

by Ida Pivoda Dunsing

Preparations for Christmas seem to be more deeply imbedded in my memory than Christmas day itself. Little girls loved their dolls and if a new one could not be included in the budget (and even if a new one was added) Mother would work long hours in the evenings mending the old ones and sewing new clothes for each one. If a china head had become broken she would somewhere find ten or fifteen cents and send me to Falutts Drug Store to choose another. The doll heads were kept on the top shelf and Mr. Crull had to climb a step ladder to reach them, a most fascinating procedure to a little girl who could barely reach the door knob to enter the store. The one I remember most vividly was the one I dropped on the sidewalk on the way home. Poor me! Poor dolly! She had to go headless for another year.

There was always a program at church a few days before Christmas. Every child in Sunday School had a part, either singing in a group or individual speaking. There was a decorated tree and at the end of the program, each child present received a bag of candy. When my oldest brother was a mid-teenager, he and his friends decided to do something very special. As in many churches, there was a small alcove behind the altar. Beginning in the alcove the boys built a portico extending out almost to the altar rail, and this they decorated beautifully with greens and other Christmas beauties. The District Superintendant happened to be visiting and he was invited to announce the speakers. One by one the children made their way to the stage, stood under the lovely portico, and said their "pieces." All went well until the Superintendant came to my brother's name, and he couldn't pronounce it so he just skipped it and went on to the next which was the closing. A horrified mumble went up among those in the know and one of the teachers had to prompt the Super and he finally announced my brother's number. It was a narrative in rhyme about the past visits of Santa Claus and how they were accomplished. All I remember of the poem is the last two lines which stated "and this year I knew the old fellow will come in a flying machine." At that a loud whirring sound was heard overhead and out of the greenery on top of the portico came the nose, then the wings of a fantastic "flying machine." A ladder was thrown out and down came old Santa with a pack on his back from which he proceeded to deliver the traditional bag of candy to each child present. The moon landing never inspired such awe as was occasioned by Grafton's first airplane. And how nearly we came to missing that momentous event because a visiting preacher couldn't pronounce a simple name like PIVODA.

Christmas Eve

by Marcia Lee Masters

The music that you heard in the stores
Is silent now.
And the gingerbread boy in the bakery window
Has lost his questioning smile:
He dreams.
The days and the weeks have blown like rain
From the pavements;
Tonight, the streets are free.

Time is a lovely thing tonight;
There are moments when it stands so still
You can catch its light in a bowl of crystal
And the sound of carols seems to come
From a world without clocks.

Take moments like these
And hold them close,
For the calm of the stars,
The peace of the fire,
And the childish hush on the stair
Were what hastened your steps
Down the crowded streets of the year.

Happy New Year!—'Are you going to make calls on New Years day?" We heard this question asked by one spruce young man of another.

We wanted to answer, for the other young man, Yes, by all means. Keep up the custom. It is eminently proper to call upon your friends and neighbors once a year, and oftener if possible.

Ladies of Ottawa, open your doors on New Years day—spread out the viands! Young men and old men of Ottawa, show your appreciation of the many entertainments the ladies have heretofore given you, by starting out early in the morning of the 1st day of 1869, for the purpose of making your neighbors and yourselves happy. Don't you quit until late in evening either.

Ottawa Republican, December 31, 1868

The Prairie Birds are busy making all due arrangements for their Annual Ball, and will soon have them completed. So they will open the holidays by a great affair. The boys are a first rate lot of fellows always on hand when there is a fire. They deserve a good turn out and will be sure to get one.

Bloomington Pantagraph, December 22, 1862

Rockford
January 5, 1879

Dear Hattie:

Mama told me that she had left New Years for me to tell about so I will. Mama had Pat take the big sleigh and all us children went out riding at half past one and stayed out about two hours. We rode down acrost the bridge and out on State street a ways, then came back and went down to the office, then up past Watson's house which was decorated with green in letters Happy New Year 1879. Willie and Hartie Humphry and I went out calling on Mama and the Ladies receiving with her at Mrs. Browns. Aunt Mame and the Ladies with her and Mrs. Dickerman and the ladies with her making in all twenty-five. I used up the rest of the cards that you and Mary gave me. Mama says that they had 125 callers. We had a turkey for dinner and squash, potatoes, jelly, bread and butter, and for dessert "Snow Pudding" and "Charlotte Russe" which was splendid.

Good night, from

Ralph

Mr. Payson's Satirical Christmas
by George Ade

Mr. Sidney Payson was full of the bitterness of Christmastide. Mr. Payson was the kind of man who loved to tell invalids that they were not looking as well as usual, and who frightened young husbands by predicting that they would regret having married. He seldom put the seal of approval on any human undertaking. It was a matter of pride with him that he never failed to find the sinister motive for the act which other people applauded. Some of his pious friends used to say that Satan had got the upper hand with him, but there were others who indicated that it might be Bile.

Think of the seething wrath and the sense of humiliation with which Mr. Sidney Payson set about his Christmas-shopping! In the first place, to go shopping for Christmas-presents was the most conventional thing that any one could do, and Mr. Payson hated conventionalities. For another thing, the giving of Christmas-presents carried with it some testimony of affection, and Mr. Payson regarded any display of affection as one of the crude symptoms of barbarous taste.

If he could have assembled his relatives at a Christmas-gathering and opened a few old family wounds, reminding his brother and his sisters of some of their youthful follies, thus shaming them before the children, Mr. Sidney Payson might have managed to make out a rather merry Christmas. Instead of that, he was condemned to go out and purchase gifts and be as cheaply idiotic as the other wretched mortals with whom he was being carried along. No wonder that he chafed and rebelled and vainly wished that he could hang crape on every Christmas-tree in the universe.

Mr. Sidney Payson hated his task and he was puzzled by it.

After wandering through two stores and looking in at twenty windows he had been unable to make one selection. It seemed to him that all the articles offered for sale were singularly and uniformly inappropriate. The custom of giving was a farce in itself, and the store-keepers had done what they could to make it a sickening travesty.

"I'll go ahead and buy a lot of things at haphazard," he said to himself. "I don't care a hang whether they are appropriate or not."

At that moment he had an inspiration. It was an inspiration which could have come to no one except Mr. Sidney Payson. It promised a speedy end to shopping hardships. It guaranteed him a Christmas to his own liking.

He was bound by family custom to buy Christmas-presents for his relatives. He had promised his sister that he would remember every one in the list. But he was under no obligation to give presents that would be welcome. Why not give to each of his relatives some present which would be entirely useless, inappropriate, and superfluous? It would serve them right for involving him in the childish performance of the Christmas-season. It would be a burlesque on the whole nonsensicality of Christmas-giving. It would irritate and puzzle his relatives and probably deepen their hatred of him. At any rate, it would be a satire on a silly tradition, and, thank goodness, it wouldn't be conventional.

Mr. Sidney Payson went into the first department-store and found himself at the book-counter.

"Have you any work which would be suitable for an elderly gentleman of studious habits and deep religious convictions?" he asked.

"We have here the works of Flavius Josephus in two volumes," replied the young woman.

"All right; I'll take them," he said. "I want them for my nephew Fred. He likes Indian stories."

The salesgirl looked at him wonderingly.

"Now, then, I want a love-story," said Mr. Payson. "I have a maiden sister who is president of a Ruskin club and writes essays about Buddhism. I want to give her a book that tells about a girl named Mabel who is loved by Sir Hector Something-or-Other. Give me a book that is full of hugs and kisses and heaving bosoms and all that sort of rot. Get just as far away from Ibsen and Howells and Henry James as you can possibly get."

"Here is a book that all the girls in the store say is very good," replied the young woman. "It is called 'Virgie's Betrothal; or, the Stranger at Birchwood Manor.' It's by Imogene Sybil Beauclerc."

"If it's what it sounds to be, it's just what I want," said Payson, showing his teeth at the young woman with a devilish glee. "You say the girls here in the store like it?"

"Yes; Miss Simmons, in the handkerchief-box department, says it's just grand."

"Ha! All right! I'll take it."

He felt his happiness rising as he went out of the store. The joy shone in his face as he stood at the skate-counter.

"I have a brother who is forty-six years old and rather fat," he said to the salesman. "I don't suppose he's been on the ice in twenty-five years. He wears a No. 9 shoe. Give me a pair of skates for him."

A few minutes later he stood at the silk-counter.

"What are those things?" he asked, pointing to some gaily coloured silks folded in boxes.

"Those are scarfs."

"Well, if you've got one that has all the colors of the rainbow in it, I'll take it. I want one with lots of yellow and red and green in it. I want something that you can hear across the street. You see, I have a sister who prides herself on her quiet taste. Her costumes are marked by what you call 'unobtrusive elegance.' I think she'd rather die than wear one of those things, so I want the biggest and noisiest one in the whole lot."

The girl didn't know what to make of Mr. Payson's strange remarks, but she was too busy to be kept wondering.

Mr. Payson's sister's husband is the president of a church temperance society, so Mr. Payson bought him a buckhorn cork-screw.

There was one more present to buy.

"Let me see," said Mr. Payson. "What is there that could be of no earthly use to a girl six years old?"

Even as he spoke his eye fell on a sign: "Bargain sale of neck-wear."

"I don't believe she would care for cravats," he said. "I think I'll buy some for her."

He saw a box of large cravats marked "25 cents each."

"Why are those so cheap?" he asked.

"Well, to tell the truth, they're out of style."

"That's good. I want eight of them—oh, any eight will do. I want them for a small niece of mine—a little girl about six years old."

Without indicating the least surprise, the salesman wrapped up the cravats.

Letters received by Mr. Sidney Payson in acknowledgment of his Christmas-presents:

I.

"Dear Brother: Pardon me for not having acknowledged the receipt of your Christmas-present. The fact is that since the skates came I have been devoting so much of my time to the re-acquiring of one of my early accomplishments that I have not had much time for writing. I wish I could express to you the delight I felt when I opened the box and saw that you had sent me a pair of skates. It was just as if you had said to me: "Will, my boy, some people may think that you are getting on in years, but I know that you're not.' I suddenly remembered that the presents which I have been receiving for several Christmases were intended for an old man. I have received easy-chairs, slippers, mufflers, smoking-jackets, and the like. When I received the pair of skates from you I felt that twenty years had been lifted off my shoulders. How in the world did you ever happen to think of them? Did you really believe that my skating-days were not over? Well, they're *not*. I went to the pond in the park on Christmas-day and worked at it for two hours and I had a lot of fun. My ankles were rather weak and I fell down twice, fortunately without any serious damage to myself or the ice, but I managed to go through the motions, and before I left I skated with a smashing pretty girl. Well, Sid, I have you to thank. I never would have ventured on skates again if it had not been for you. I was a little stiff yesterday, but this morning I went out again and had a dandy time. I owe the renewal of my youth to you. Thank you many times, and believe me to be, as ever, your affectionate brother,

"WILLIAM."

2.

"Dear Brother: The secret is out! I suspected it all the time. It is needless for you to offer denial. Sometimes when you have acted the cynic I have almost believed that you were sincere, but each time I have been relieved to observe in you something which told me that underneath your assumed indifference there was a genial current of the romantic sentiment of the youth and the lover. How can I be in doubt after receiving a little book—a love-story?

"I knew, Sidney dear, that you would remember me at Christmas. You have always been the soul of thoughtfulness, especially to those of us who understood you. I must confess, however, that I expected you to do the deadly conventional thing and send me something heavy and serious. I knew it would be a book. All of my friends send me books. That comes of being president of a literary club. But you are the only one, Sidney, who had the rare and kindly judgment to appeal to the woman and not to the club president. Because I am interested in a serious literary movement it need not follow that I want my whole life to be overshadowed by the giants of the kingdom of letters. Although I would not dare confess it to Mrs. Peabody or Mrs. Hutchens, there are times when I like to spend an afternoon with an old-fashioned love-story.

"You are a bachelor, Sidney, and as for me, I have long since ceased to blush at the casual mention of 'old maid.' It was not for us to know the bitter-sweet experiences of courtship and marriage, and you will remember that we have sometimes pitied the headlong infatuation of sweethearts and have felt rather superior in our freedom. And yet, Sidney, if we chose to be perfectly candid with each other, I dare say that both of us would confess to having known something about that which men call *love*. We might confess that we had felt its subtle influence, at times and places, and with a stirring uneasiness, as one detects a draught. We might go so far as to admit that sometimes we pause in our lonely lives and wonder what might have been and whether it would not have been better, after all. I am afraid that I am writing like a sentimental school-girl, but you must know that I have been reading your charming little book, and it has come to me as a message from you. Is it not really a confession, Sidney?

"You have made me very happy, dear brother. I feel more closely drawn to you than at any time since we were all together at Christmas, at the old home. Come and see me. Your loving sister,

"GERTRUDE."

3.

"Dear Brother: Greetings to you from the happiest household in town, thanks to a generous Santa Claus in the guise of Uncle Sidney. I must begin by thanking you on my own account. How in the world did you ever learn that Roman colors had come in again? I have always heard that men did not follow the styles and could not be trusted to select anything for a woman, but it is a libel, a base libel, for the scarf which you sent is quite the most *beautiful* thing I have received this Christmas. I have it drapped over the large picture in the parlor, and it is the envy of every one who has been in today. A *thousand, thousand* thanks, dear Sidney. It was perfectly sweet of you to remember me, and I call it nothing less than a stroke of genius to think of anything so appropriate and yet so much out of the ordinary.

"John asks me to thank you—but I must tell you the story. One evening last week we had a little chafing-dish party after prayer-meeting, and I asked John to open a bottle of olives for me. Well, he broke the small blade of his knife trying to get the cork out. He said: 'If I live to get downtown again, I'm going to buy a corkscrew.' Fortunately he had neglected to buy one, and so your gift seemed to come straight from Providence. John is very much pleased. Already he has found use for it, as it happened that he wanted to open a bottle of household ammonia the very first thing this morning.

"As for Fred's lovely books, thank goodness you didn't send him any more story-books. John and I have been trying to induce him to take up a more serious line of reading. The Josephus ought to help him in the study of his Sunday-school lessons. We were pleased to observe that he read it for about an hour this morning.

"When you were out here last fall did Genevieve tell you that she was collecting silk for a doll quilt? She insists that she did not, but she must have done so, for how could you have guessed that she wants pieces of silk above anything else in the world? The perfectly lovely cravats which you sent will more than complete the quilt, and I think that mamma will get some of the extra pieces for herself. Fred and Genevieve send love and kisses. John insists that you come out to dinner some Sunday very soon—next Sunday if you can. After we received your presents we were quite ashamed of the box we had sent over to your hotel, but we will try to make up the difference in heart-felt gratitude. Don't forget—any Sunday. Your loving sister.

"KATHERINE."

It would be useless to tell what Mr. Payson thought of himself after he received these letters.

George Ade, 1866-1944, was a Chicago newspaper humorist who worked for years on the staff of the Morning News, *and authored more than thirty books and plays.*

The Snow Fall
by Archibald MacLeish

Quietness clings to the air.
Quietness gathers the bell
To a great distance.
Listen!
This is the snow.
This is the slow
Chime
The snow
Makes.
It encloses us.
Time in the snow is alone:
Time in the snow is at last,
Is past.

Born in 1892 in Glencoe to parents prominent in Illinois educational and merchant life Archibald MacLeish, poet, dramatist, professor, and Librarian of Congress, won several Pulitzer prizes for his work.

Christmas on the Roof of the World
by Ernest Hemingway

While it was still dark, Ida, the little German maid, came in and lit the fire in the big porcelain stove, and the burning pine wood roared up the chimney.

Out the window the lake lay steel gray far down below, with the snow-covered mountains bulking jagged beyond it, and far away beyond it the massive tooth of the Dent du Midi beginning to lighten with the first touch of morning.

It was so cold outside. The air felt like something alive as I drew a deep breath. You could swallow the air like a drink of cold water.

I reached up with a boot and banged on the ceiling.

"Hey, Chink. It's Christmas!"

"Hooray!" came Chink's voice down from the little room under the roof of the chalet.

Herself was up in a warm, woollen dressing-robe, with the heavy goat's wool ski-ing socks.

Chink knocked at the door.

"Merry Christmas, mes enfants," he grinned. He wore the early morning garb of big, woolly dressing-robe and thick socks that made us all look like some monastic order.

In the breakfast-room we could hear the stove roaring and crackling. Herself opened the door.

Against the tall, white porcelain stove hung the three long ski-ing stockings, bulging and swollen with strange lumps and bulges. Around the foot of the stove were piled boxes. Two new shiny pairs of ash skis lay alongside the stove, too tall to stand in the low-ceilinged chalet room.

For a week we had each been making mysterious trips to the Swiss town below on the lake. Hadley and I, Chink and I, and Hadley and Chink, returning after dark with strange boxes and bundles that were concealed in various parts of the chalet. Finally we each had to make a trip alone. That was yesterday. Then last night we had taken turns on the stockings, each pledged not to sleuth.

Chink had spent every Christmas since 1914 in the army. He was our best friend. For the first time in years it seemed like Christmas to all of us.

We ate breakfast in the old, untasting, gulping, early morning Christmas way, unpacked the stockings, down to the candy mouse in the toe, each made a pile of our things for future gloating.

From breakfast we rushed into our clothes and tore down the icy road in the glory of the blue-white glistening alpine morning. The train was just pulling out. Chink and I shot the skis into the baggage car, and we all three swung aboard.

All Switzerland was on the move. Ski-ing parties, men, women, boys and girls, taking the train up the mountain, wearing their tight-fitting blue caps, the girls all in riding-breeches and puttees, and shouting and calling out to one another. Platforms jammed.

Everybody travels third class in Swirtzerland, and on a big day like Christmas the third class overflows and the overflow is crowded into the sacred red plush first class compartments.

Shouting and cheering the train crawled alongside the mountain, climbing up towards the top of the world.

There was no big Christmas dinner at noon in Switzerland. Everybody was out in the mountain air with a lunch in the rucksack and the prospect of the dinner at night.

When the train reached the highest point it made in the mountains, everybody piled out, the stacks of skis were unsorted from the baggage-car and transferred to an open flat car hooked on a jerky little train that ran straight up the side of the mountain on cog wheels.

At the top we could look over the whole world, white, glistening in the powder snow, and ranges of mountains stretching off in every direction.

It was the top of a bob sled run that looped and turned in icy windings far below. A bob shot past, all the crew moving in time, and as it rushed at express train speed for the first turn, the crew all cried, "Ga-a-a-a-r!" and the bob roared in an icy smother around the curve and dropped off down the glassy run below.

No matter how high you are in the mountains there is always a slope going up.

There were long strips of seal-skin harnessed on our skis, running back from the tip to the base in a straight strip with the grain of the hair pointing back, so that you pushed right ahead through the snow going up hill. If your skis had a tendency to slide back the slipping movement would be checked by the seal skin hairs. They would slide smoothly forward, but hold fast at the end of each thrusting stride.

Soon the three of us were high above the shoulder of the mountain that had seemed the top of the world. We kept going up in single file, sliding smoothly up through the snow in a long upward zig-zag.

We passed through the last of the pines and came out on a shelving plateau. Here came the first run-down—a half-mile sweep ahead. At the brow the skis seemed to drop out from under and in a hissing rush we all three swooped down the slope like birds.

On the other side it was thrusting, uphill, steady climbing again. The sun was hot and the sweat poured off us in the steady up-hill drive. There is no place you get so tanned as in the mountains in winter. Nor so hungry. Nor so thirsty.

Finally we hit the lunching place, a snowed-under old log cattle barn where the peasant's cattle would shelter in the summer when this mountain was green with pasture. Everything seemed to drop off sheer below us.

The air at that height, about 6,200 feet, is like wine. We put on our sweaters that had been in our ruck-sacks coming up, unpacked the lunch and the bottle of white wine, and lay back on our ruck-sacks and soaked in the sun. Coming up we had been wearing sun glasses against the glare of the snowfields, and now we took off the amber shaded goggles and looked out on a bright, new world.

"I'm really too hot," Herself said. Her face had burned coming up, even through the last crop of freckles and tan.

"You ought to use lampblack on your face," Chink suggested.

But there is no record of any woman that has ever yet been willing to use that famous mountaineer's specific against snow-blindness and sun-burn.

It was no time after lunch and Herself's daily nap, while Chink and I practised turns and stops on the slope, before the heat was gone out of the sun and it was time to start down. We took off the seal skins and waxed our skis.

Then in one long, dropping, swooping, heart-plucking rush we were off. A seven-mile run down and no sensation in the world that can compare with it. You do not make the seven miles in one run. You go as fast as you believe possible, then you go a good deal faster, then you give up all hope, then you don't know what happened, but the earth came up and over and over and you sat up and untangled yourself from your skis and looked around. Usually all three had spilled together. Sometimes there was no one in sight.

But there is no place to go except down. Down in a rushing, swooping, flying, plunging rush of fast ash blades through the powder snow.

Finally, in a rush we came out on to the road on the shoulder of the mountain where the cog-wheel railway had stopped coming up. Now we were all a shooting stream of ski-ers. All the Swiss were coming down, too. Shooting along the road in a seemingly endless stream.

It was too steep and slippery to stop. There was nothing to do but plunge along down the road as helpless as though you were in a mill race. So we went down. Herself was way ahead somewhere. We could see her blue beret occasionally before it got too dark.

Down, down, down the road we went in the dusk, past chalets that were a burst of lights and Christmas merriment in the dark.

Then the long line of ski-ers shot into the black woods, swung to one side to avoid a team and sledge coming up the road, passed more chalets, their windows alight with the candles from the Christmas trees. As we dropped past a chalet, watching nothing but the icy road and the man ahead, we heard a shout from the lighted doorway.

"Captain! Captain! Stop here!"

It was the German-Swiss landlord of our chalet. We were running past it in the dark.

Ahead of us, spilled at the turn, we found Herself and we stopped in a sliding slither, knocking loose our skis, and the three of us hiked up the hill towards the lights of the chalet. The lights looked very cheerful against the dark pines of the hill, and inside was a big Christmas tree and a real Christmas turkey dinner, the table shiny with silver, the glasses tall and thin stemmed, the bottles narrow-necked, the turkey large and brown and beautiful, the side dishes all present, and Ida serving in a new crisp apron.

It was the kind of a Christmas you can only get on top of the world.

Ernest Hemingway was born and educated in Oak Park. He won the Nobel Prize for literature in 1954.

Celebrating
the Nativity

Christmas Eve
by Eugene Field

Oh, hush thee, little Dear-my-soul,
    The evening shades are falling—
Hush thee, my dear, dost thou not hear
    The voice of the Master calling?

Deep lies the snow upon the earth,
    But all the sky is ringing
With joyous song, and all night long
    The stars shall dance, with singing.

Oh hush thee, little Dear-my-soul,
    And close thine eyes in dreaming,
And angels fair shall lead thee where
    The singing stars are beaming.

A shepherd calls his little lambs,
    And he longeth to caress them;
He bids them rest upon his breast,
    That his tender love may bless them.

So hush thee, little Dear-my-soul,
    Whilst evening shades are falling,
And above the song of the heavenly throng
    Thou shalt hear the Master calling.

Chicago journalist well known in the late 19th century for his "Sharps and Flats" newspaper column, Eugene Field wrote a number of poems and stories about Christmas, his most famous being "Jest 'Fore Christmas."

Always the Young Stranger
by Carl Sandburg

At Christmas the Old Man brought home and gave to each of us a five-cent bag of candy, a large five-cent orange, and some present like a toy, a knife, or a muffler. And we knew it was a Hard Times Christmas when the father gave us each only a five-cent bag of candy, a large five-cent orange, and a long sad look. We honored the oranges by eating all the insides, pulp and peelings.

It was early to bed on Christmas Eve and everybody up at four-thirty in the morning for Julotta services in church at five o'clock. I remember walking one Christmas morning with my hand in my father's hand. It was on Chambers Street near Mulberry and opposite the old Acme Mill. I had been reading in the books about stars and I had this early morning been taking a look now and then up at a sky of clear stars. And at this place where a driveway went out onto Chambers Street, I turned my face up toward my father's and said, pointing with the loose hand, "You know, some of those stars are millions of miles away." And my father, without looking down toward me, gave a sniff, as though I was a funny little fellow, and said, "We won't bodder about dat now, Sholly." For several blocks neither of us said a word and I felt, while still holding his hand, that there were millions of empty miles between us.

What would the mother have said? After smiling softly to me probably these exact words, which I heard often from her: "It is an interesting world we live in—full of the wonders God has made for us to think about."

Star Silver

by Carl Sandburg

The silver of one star
Plays cross-lights against pine green.

And the play of this silver
Crosswise against the green
Is an old story . . .
                    thousands of years.

And sheep raisers on the hills by night
Watching the wooly four-footed ramblers,
Watching a single silver star—
Why does the story never wear out?

And a baby slung in a feed-box
Back in a barn in a Bethlehem slum,
A baby's first cry mixing with the crunch
Of a mule's teeth on Bethlehem Christmas corn,
Baby fists softer than snowflakes of Norway,
The vagabond mother of Christ
And the vagabond men of wisdom,
All in a barn on a winter night,
And a baby there in swaddling clothes on hay—
Why does the story never wear out?

The sheen of it all
Is a star silver and a pine green
For the heart of a child asking a story,
The red and hungry, red and hankering heart
Calling for cross-lights of silver and green.

Carl Sandburg, born in Galesburg in 1878, stayed close to his Illinois roots in his poetry, collections of folksongs and children's stories, as well as his six volume biography of Lincoln. He is one of America's most celebrated poets.

Christmas 1956

by Rev. Frank Hobart Millett

How oft at Christmastime before
I've knelt without the stable door
    Mine eyes and ears to strain—
But only children see the star
And hear the voices from afar
    And sing the glad refrain.

Again I kneel my gift to bring,
And from a heart that fain would sing
    Just one request is wrung:
Though thronging years go hastening by,
And golden sunset tints the sky,
    Lord, keep me ever young.

Trinity Church, Wheaton

Lonigan at Midnight Mass

by James T. Farrell

The choir sang the appointed psalm. A sense of solemnity came upon Studs. He bowed his head as Father Doneggan reverently lifted the paten before the crucifix. Studs' head remained bowed. A vision of Heaven, with God enthroned in red on a golden throne, came to him as through a mist. He was unaware of the sacred progress of the mass, and he knelt with his head still bowed, filled with vague thoughts of adoration, until he heard the choir:

The shepherds were watching, the whole night through,
Under the starry sky. . . .

As a boy, he had sung the song in the children's choir at five o'clock mass on Christmas morning. The feeling of Christmas, a feeling of joy and reverence suffused upon him, and he remembered boyhood Christmas days, with the snow coming down as he dashed to five o'clock mass, wearing high, laced boots like those lumberjacks wore in movies, kicking chunks of ice with them, hoping to meet Lucy, meeting Dan and Bill, hunching his face forwards and hurrying into a raw wind. He remembered himself, Dan and Bill running to church to be there on time. He remembered them singing, with Lucy, standing with the girls, singing, now and then seeming to dart a glance at him, and TB McCarthy in front of him, goofily singing:

The shepherds were guzzling the whole night through,
Under the beery sky. . . .

The tune of the Christmas song ran through his mind, again drawing it back to boyhood, and boyhood Christmas days, and that Christmas morning that he had come home from five o'clock mass, and had been given a ten dollar gold piece by his old man, and in the afternoon, he and Dan Donoghue had gone to a show and seen Salome, with Theda Bara as Salome. He was sad because he had grown up, and because the years passed like a river that no man could stop. Oh, come let us adore, oh, come let us adore, Christ, Our King. He had all the old feelings he had used to have on Christmas day, feelings he could not find words for, feelings that ran through the songs sung in church on Christmas. . . .

The bell knelled through the hushed church. Studs bowed his head in unison with the people, and tapped his breast. His thoughts were vague. His body and mind seemed separated, his mind swimming away free and in a sea of melancholy, his body heavy and sluggish like a dragging weight.

He listened to the choir singing, a sweetness and strength in their voices and in the song:

Agnus Dei, qui tollis peccata mundi. . . .

He watched Father Doneggan bowing his head low and silently reciting the prayers in immediate preparation for the reception of Holy Communion. Through his mind there ran a communion song;

Oh, Lord, I am not worthy,
That Thou shouldst come to me.
But speak the words of comfort,
And my spirit healed shall be.

Chicago native James T. Farrell has chronicled life among 20th century lower middle class Irish Americans in numerous novels. Studs Lonigan, from which this brief excerpt is taken, is considered a modern classic.

Three Million Sang Carols, 1924

Chicago, this city with a record of doing things in a big way, lived up to its reputation this Christmas with the greatest civic musical demonstration in history in the singing of Christmas carols on the largest scale ever heard in the world.

This noteworthy movement to spread the spirit of good will to men was started last Christmas and proved a wonderful success. With the advantage of this experience, the Chicago Christmas Carols committee, of which Harry Edward Freund, of the Music Research bureau, who was the originator of the movement, is director, completed the arrangements for this year's musical festival which dwarfed last year's celebration.

"More than 2,000,000 copies of the five Christmas carols sung this Christmas were printed and distributed by the committee, which distributes the songs free, this number being twice as many as last year," said Mr. Freund, in a report made public here. "This fact, together with the unanimous enthusiasm shown in singing the carols in hotel lobbies, clubs, churches, hospitals, institutions, places of business, and almost every other place where people gather, makes plain that the citizens of Chicago have adopted civic carol singing as the annual expression of the spirit of the city.

More than 3,000,000 people in Chicago and in the metropolitan district surrounding it participated in this wonderful expression of cheer at Christmastime.

Christmas Carol
by Sara Teasdale

The kings they came from out the south,
    All dressed in ermine fine;
They bore Him gold and chrysoprase,
    And gifts of precious wine.

The shepherds came from out the north,
    Their coats were brown and old;
They brought Him little new-born lambs—
    They had not any gold.

The wise men came from out the east,
    And they were wrapped in white;
The star that led them all the way
    Did glorify the night.

The angels came from heaven high,
    And they were clad with wings;
And lo, they brought a joyful song
    The host of heaven sings.

The kings they knocked upon the door,
    The wise men entered in,
The shepherds followed after them
    To hear the song begin.

The angels sang through all the night
    Until the rising sun,
But little Jesus fell asleep
    Before the song was done.

Born in St. Louis, Sara Teasdale was very much a part of the Chicago literary group mentored by Harriet Monroe's Poetry *magazine.*

The World's Fair at Chicago will be the great event of 1893. All the world and his wife will be going to the Exhibition. Few questions will be more generally discussed this Christmas at family gatherings than the attraction of the Chicago trip.

William T. Stead, Mowbray House, England

A Bohemian Christmas in Chicago
Clara Ingram Judson

As days grew shorter and Christmas neared, the Kovec cottage was full of secrets and fragrant odors. The minute Anna and Rosie got home from school, they put on big aprons and helped with baking. Two great stone jars, bought to replace the pair that had to be left in Prague, were already half full of spicy goodies. This day the mother was making the decorated *dorts*.

"Papa and Jan will like these pastries," Rosie remarked gleefully as she washed her hands and tied on her apron. She was careful to say nothing about her own sweet tooth—if she was very helpful, perhaps her mamma would let her eat one when the pastries came from the oven. She fetched the rolling board and pin, got the jar of raisins, and began seeding them without being told.

"These are going to be the best I've ever made," Mrs. Kovec predicted. "I'll make a big, big batch too. Anna will be here with the marketing soon. Your papa and Jan went up to the city and will be late. We have plenty of time. Quince is cooked—with cinnamon and ginger as your papa likes it. If you think you can do it nicely, maybe I'll let you put pastry strips on top of a few apple *dorts* and we'll have those for supper."

"Oh, I can, Mamma! I'll make them the prettiest we ever had!" Rosie watched her mother's skillful fingers mix and mold the dough.

"Now then," her mother said, as she picked up the rolling pin, "tell me the Christmas poem. Tell it in English, Rosie, every word."

When Anna arrived with the marketing, Rosie was reciting English words:

"'Twas the night before Christmas and all through the house,
Not a creature was stirring, not even a mouse."

Anna set the basket down and recited with Rosie:

" "The stockings were hung by the chimney with care,
     In hopes that Saint Nicholas soon would be there.' "

"My teacher says Saint Nicholas doesn't ever come on his day—not in America," Anna remarked. "That's why you were disappointed, Rosie." Poor Rosie! She had hung up her stocking, as always, on December sixth—Saint Nicholas' Day, which Bohemian children call "Saint Mikulas' Day"—but next morning there it hung, limp and empty. Papa had been indifferent to her disappointment.

"Didn't I tell you that in America, December sixth is nothing? Nothing but another day! Didn't I tell you that in America, Saint Nick comes on Christmas Eve?"

"Not till then?" Rosie had been anxious and disappointed for days. She had not quite believed this postponement.

Now she whirled on Anna, her outstretched hands sticky with raisins.

"You think he will come Christmas Eve, don't you, Anna?" she asked eagerly.

"I'm certain of it!" Anna said. Why shouldn't she be certain? She had been knitting mittens diligently after Rosie went to sleep, mittens with a snowflake pattern across the back, just what Rosie would like. Jan was carving a wooden doll and painting on it an excellent face that smiled mischievously, and Mamma had made a whole new outfit for the doll. American clothes, very stylish. But of course Rosie knew nothing of this, though she did notice that her family took sudden interest in getting her to bed. Unfortunately, she was never able to keep awake and see what they were up to.

"I'm as sure Saint Nick is coming as—as—I am that we're making pastries. You hang up your stocking Christmas Eve!" By now Anna had her apron on and was at work too.

When Jan and his father returned about eight o'clock, the house was full of the smell of sugar and spice and browning fruit juices. They sniffed hungrily. It was a good thing Anna had the supper ready, and that the decorated tarts were put out of sight. Otherwise, many might have been eaten up then and there.

Later, when hunger was satisfied, Kovec sat back in his chair and remarked, "How would you like a treat tomorrow evening?"

"Tomorrow!" Anna said, "Tomorrow is Saturday." She had looked forward to Saturday all week, for that was the time when she worked at the music shop.

"Tomorrow," Kovec said, and he was not thinking of a music shop. He winked at Jan like a conspirator, and they grinned at each other. "How would you like to go to the city?"

"Already we are in Chicago," Anna said, wondering what he was planning.

"Yes, Chicago," Kovec agreed, "But now I mean State Street the fine stoes, the bright lights."

"And get Jan's face cut by those gangs?" Mrs. Kovec retorted.

Jan waved that aside. "No danger now, Mamma. A Bohemian is on the City Council."

"Frank Dvorak is an American," Kovec corrected Jan. "If he wasn't an American, he couldn't be elected to the council."

"Yes," Jan agreed. "But he is Bohemian-born. The first to be elected to a city office. You told me yourself. Papa. He is trying to make people understand us. He says that is the way to stop fights. Miss Jane Addams helps him. There's no danger now, Mamma."

Mrs. Kovec began to stack the dishes and clear a place for newspapers.

"Well, maybe," she granted.

"Where are these bright lights, Papa?" Rosie asked.

"In the store windows. On the streets. Oh, there are so many you shall see tomorrow, Rosicka."

The next day as soon as Anna got home, the Kovecs set out for the city. Rosie held her father's hand and skipped briskly to keep up with him. "I can say some new words, Papa," she boasted.

"Do I know them?" he asked, half teasing her.

"You never said them, Papa—not that I've heard."

"Then tell me!"

"'Merry Christmas!' Guess what that means!"

"Well, what?"

"*Vesele Vanoce!*" Rosie answered. "It is the same, my teacher says. So this year I shall wake you up and tell you 'Merry Christmas,' and now you'll know what it means, Papa."

"*Vesele Vanoce!* Merry Christmas!" Mrs. Kovec repeated. "Only the sound of the words is different."

"The verses too," Papa said. "Tell them now while we walk." So Rosie said twelve Christmas verses on the way to the stores.

"Since the elevated is getting built," Kovec told them soon, "this part of the city is called 'The Loop' because the tracks go around and around." He swung his arms about, but the others paid little heed to his information, for at that minute they turned into State Street.

The wonder of that sight made their eyes open. Horses drawing handsome carriages clattered over cobblestone streets. Great drays, some pulled by double mule teams, some by enormous horses, were piled high with packing cases. Window displays glittered. Getting across the street was an exciting adventure, with everyone in fine spirits. The policeman at the corner helped Mrs. Kovec to the curb and grinned at Rosie. In all the crowds, no one seemed cross or hateful—people hurried by, smiling, laden with parcels, laughing because Christmas was near. The fragrance of pine and blazing candles scented the air and added to the holiday feeling.

Anna was too thrilled for talk. State Street was a beautiful sight—buildings, higher than any in Prague, were so tall that roofs were lost in the sky. No wonder Papa calls them "skyscrapers!" she thought. Windows glowed brightly. Each tall building was like a great box, punctured with tiny holes and stood on end, with a candle burning inside. Anna had made such a box many a time, but never had she thought to see a likeness so vast in size.

"Come this way—through the crowd, if you want to look in the windows," Papa said.

Anna wanted to linger at each window, but her father dragged them on.

"You have something special to show us, Papa?" Anna guessed when he had pulled her away from a window display of musical instruments.

"That's right!" he admitted. "Now come—in the next block!" He took her arm, and Rosie's on his other side. Jan was looking after his mother.

"There, look!" He stopped in front of a great window. The girls stared in wonder. Jan, who had seen it before but had kept it a secret, was as pleased as they were.

On the floor of the store window was the model of a small city. At least, it seemed to be a city, Anna thought. She saw buildings, many, many buildings, some large, some small, all gleaming white. Walks were threadlike lines between tiny gardens. Boats of various sorts—tiny steamers, gondolas, canoes, barges—floated on mirror lakes. Tiny flags of many sorts fluttered from turreted roofs. Little people, men, women, and children dressed smartly in fashion, strolled on the walks, crossed on bridges, descended wide, white steps.

"Is it fairyland?" Rosie whispered, awed by the lovely sight.

"That is a model of the World's Fair," her father told her. He said the words proudly, as though he had had a part in the wonder himself.

"'World's Fair?'" Anna repeated his words.

"Some call it the Columbian Exposition, some the White City," Kovec told her. "World's Fair is good enough for me." He spoke all these words in English. Indeed, the more her father worked with men in the city, the more he spoke English and the easier his words came.

"Shall we see it, Papa?" Anna asked.

"Oh, yes!" Kovec spoke with sureness.

"Did I tell you that Mr. Pakos says Dvorak will come to play?" Anna wondered.

Jan grinned at her. She had told everything about that evening with Mr. Pakos a dozen times over.

"Rosie! You were to select a new star for our Christmas tree—remember. Papa? We'd better hurry or the stores will close." Jan dragged her away from the enchanting window.

From that evening the days raced by until Christmas. Friday Jan had no work, and he was glad of that, for he was needed at home. He bought a little Christmas tree on Blue Island Avenue and fixed a firm base for it in a corner of the front room. He fixed a great stack of wood for his mother. Cousins from the northwest side, the Kafkas, whom they had not seen since arriving, were having Christmas Eve dinner at the Kovecs'. With the Dubecs, that would make a big party to entertain.

Anna unpacked the manger scene, brought from Prague, and set it up under the tree. Mamma cooked a big supper for Friday, because Saturday, the twenty-fourth, the family would fast until the evening star came out. Rosie thought this was a terrible ordeal and began complaining even as she was setting Friday's supper table.

"Think of all we'll be doing," Anna tried to divert her. "We'll take down the big bed. We'll put up a long table in the front room. Mamma will set the bread and make the *bousky*."

This was a favorite sweet bread with chopped, candied fruits inside. "She has started the roe soup and stuffed the goose, already."

"Wouldn't there be a little crumb of something I could eat?" Rosie teased.

"Not a morsel!" her mother said, vexed at the teasing. "What's come over you, Rosie?"

"Maybe tomorrow you will really see the Golden Pig," Jan encouraged Rosie. "Remember Grandma always said that if you didn't eat a crumb all day, you'd surely see the Pig—and that means luck for a whole year?"

"I would rather have food than luck," Rosie replied. "Anyway, I'm lucky enough."

"You're in luck now," Jan laughed, "because you're going to help me tie candles on this tree. Wait, I'll climb on a chair and you pass them to me."

Finally Christmas Eve arrived. Errands were done; the table looked sumptuous—almost every inch was covered with good food. The tree with the manger scene below was perfect.

"Don't muss the curtains, Rosie," Mrs. Kovec said nervously. She looked around to see that everything was right.

"I'm looking for the evening star, Mamma!" Rosie cried. "I see it! I see it! Look!" She let the starched lace curtains drop and ran to the table, "Now may I have a *dort*?"

"Wait till Anna brings the light, Rosicka," her mother said. "When I was a little girl, we didn't hurry to end the fasting. We watched the ceiling patiently after we saw the evening star, knowing that if we glimpsed the shadow of the Golden Pig up there, we'd have luck and plenty for a year."

Anna lighted the lamp in the kitchen and slowly walked into the front room. Rosie peered at the ceiling, watching dusky shadows flit across as Anna moved.

"I see it! I see it, Anna," the little girl shouted, dancing up and down and clapping her hands. "He's there—no! Anna, you moved! Now he's gone! But I did see the Golden Pig this time, I did, Mamma."

Anna set the lamp on the shelf. Mrs. Kovec studied the table for anything forgotten, Papa came hurrying in, and the guests were at the door. The Christmas celebration had begun.

Getting Ready for Christmas
by Rowena Bennett

Who's getting ready for Christmas tonight?
"I," said the snow, "I have turned the world white."
"I," said the frost, "with my magical mixture
I've painted on everyone's window a picture."
"I," said the forester, bringing home fuel,
"I've gathered faggots and logs for the Yule."
"I," said the cook. "I have roasted a pheasant
And cooked a great boar's head to make the feast pleasant."
"I," said the minstrel, "I've made up a ballad
To sing to the king while he's eating his salad. . . ."

Who's getting ready for holiday mirth?
Why! All happy children all over the earth!

The poetry of Rowena Bennett, born in 1896, appeared in popular children's and adult periodicals such as St. Nicholas Magazine *and the* Saturday Review of Literature.

They Traveled from Afar
by Harold Blake Walker

The Wise Men caught sight of Christ's star in the East. Curiously, there were thousands of others who did not see the star. Probably they were not looking for it. Maybe they were so bogged down in their shops, trying to make ends meet, or so busy with their affairs and their engagements it had not occurred to them to look up. We never see the stars when we have our eyes focused on our plodding feet, our heads bowed and our shoulders sagging.

Somebody remarked the other day that the common run of television actors seem utterly uninspired, mired in the mediocre, as if they were just going through the required motions and saying the necessary lines. They seem to have lost sight of the star. Yet most of them, I dare say, were dreamers once. They had visions of greatness. They were eager to reveal something ultimate about life in their acting and their speaking. Possibly life, and the struggle for a place, wore them down and eroded their dreams. Now there's no life in acting insipid scenes and saying uninspired lines.

It is strange how easily that happens to us. Life wears us down unless some star lures us beyond our little hurts and disappointments. There's always something, a washed-out bridge or a landslide, a business failure or an illness, to thwart our dreams. Somebody always is saying, "If only this or that were different I could succeed and be happy." But it just isn't so. What is outside never is the measure of triumph or of defeat. Now and then, like Martha in *The Winthrop Woman*, we feel as if we are "made of cobweb that tears at a touch," but even Martha could manage the rigors of pioneer life and endure to help found this land of ours.

Henry Thoreau put his finger on the source of joy and triumph in life when he remarked, "Making the earth say beans instead of grass—this was my daily work." Making life say something creative, something worthwhile is our daily work. Paul had been trying to make his life say Christ and the world had assailed him with its utter disbelief. But, as the great apostle said, "I was not disobedient to the heavenly vision."

Trouble comes into life, sometimes devastating and crushing, and with our shoulders sagging life seems to be "a nightmare between two nothings." But when the star still shines for us, and we go on making the earth say "beans instead of grass," life is, as Browning wrote,

". . . just a stuff
To try the soul's strength, educe the man."

What life does to us, whether it leads us to believe our struggles are "just a nightmare between two nothings," or reveals the soul's strength and creates the man, depends on whether it finds in us some "heavenly vision," some star whose challenge will not let us go.

Who can doubt the joy of Father Chisholm in A.J. Cronin's *The Keys of the Kingdom* struggling against odds as a missionary in China. He put the clue to his courage and radiance in his remark to Shang-Foo, whose garden was washed away by a seasonal flood. "My plantings are all lost," Foo gloomed. "We shall have to begin all over again." And Father Chisholm replied, "That is life . . . to begin again when everything is lost." But who can begin again when everything is lost without the challenge of a star?

Star of My Heart
by Vachel Lindsay

Star of my heart, I follow from afar.
Sweet Love on high, lead on where shepherds are,
Where Time is not, and only dreamers are.
Star from of old, the Magi-Kings are dead
And a foolish Saxon seeks the manger-bed.
O lead me to Jehovah's child
Across this dreamland lone and wild,
Then I will speak this prayer unsaid,
And kiss his little haloed head—
"My star and I, we love thee, little child."

Except the Christ be born again to-night
In dreams of all men, saints and sons of shame,
The world will never see his kingdom bright.
Star of all hearts, lead onward thro' the night
Past death-black deserts, doubts without a name,
Past hills of pain and mountains of new sin
To that far sky where mystic births begin,
Where dreaming ears the angel-song shall win.
Our Christmas shall be rare at dawning there,
And each shall find his brother fair,
Like a little child within:
All hearts of the earth shall find new birth
And wake, no more to sin.

Springfield native Vachel Lindsay, born in 1879, vagabond poet and artist, was one of the writers of the Chicago literary group. In the decade preceding the first World War he was perhaps America's most prominent poet.

Babushka

by Katharine Gibson

Late one snowy night in Russia, more than nineteen hundred years ago, Babushka was sweeping her house. She was the best housekeeper in the village. And though she lived all by herself, her little cottage was as bright as a new kopék. Even though it was winter, flowers bloomed on her window sill. Her painted walls were as gay as when the colors were still wet, her carved doorway, her carved bed, her little carved chairs were waxed and polished until they shone like the soft satin of some great lady's gown. From morn to sundown Babushka was at work in her tiny house, so it is no wonder that she was sweeping late at night.

When she had finished she opened her door to brush the snow from her sill. The moon shone brightly, the snow lay heaped like silver and the ice of the river gleamed like a string of brilliant crystals. The wind blew sharply; it cut through Babushka's little furred dress and nipped her ears and nose until they were scarlet.

Suddenly a warmth came into the wind; it seemed like a spring breeze; it was filled with the most delicious fragrance. "What could it be?" Babushka wondered. "Where does it come from?"

She looked down the road. There in the shining moonlight was the most marvelous procession she had ever seen. First there came an outrider on a strange, long-legged, humped beast which she later learned was a camel. The outrider had a long curved sword. His mantle was of scarlet. Silently he came; his beast's padded feet made no noise. Following him was an endless line of horsemen all arrayed in strange armor from the east. Each of these was followed by a servant bearing a torch. The torch flared out dimly in the moonlight. The hoofs of the horses sank deeply into the snow. They were also silent.

Behind the riders came carts filled with all manner of folk, dressed as gayly as gypsies though they were in silks and cloth of gold, not in rags. They had tents striped red and blue, finely woven rugs; they had cooking pots of brass and copper rimmed with silver, dishes of silver, and jeweled drinking cups. All of these flashed brilliantly. Babushka could hardly believe her wondering eyes. On came the procession; cart after cart sank into the deep snow; silently they moved. At last the end! There rode Three Men, the most wonderful she had ever gazed upon.

One was little and old, he had gray hair beneath his turban, his beard was gray, but his dim eyes were young with watching. He was dressed from head to foot in a garment of gold, the color of the rising sun.

One was somewhat taller and younger; his eyes were bright; his hair curled crisply. He was robed in silk the color of evening, violet and purple.

Then came the Third. Never in all her life had Babushka seen any man so tall. His face was as beautiful as though it had been cut from an old coin; his skin was black. He was an Ethiopian. He was wearing the color of the noonday sun, orange and flame.

The First of the three held gold in his hand; the Second and Third had small caskets from which issued the warm, delicious fragrance that had first greeted Babushka's eager nostrils.

Babushka lifted her eyes to the Three. At first they did not see her. The Ethiopian was pointing to the heavens; the others were looking where he pointed. Babushka gazed too. Right above the Three was a star. It was so bright that it dazzled Babushka's eyes. Even the moon seemed pale beside its marvelous, streaming rays. As Babushka stood there in front of her door in her little furred gown, with the light from the lamps making a crown of her dark braids, she was very fair. The First Man gave a signal; the whole procession stopped; as it did so, the star stood still above them. The Second spoke.

"Do you watch the star, also?"

Babushka was so amazed and so filled by the music of his voice that she could only bow and curtsy.

"It leads us to the King," said the First.

"Will you not go with us?" spoke the Ethiopian. "We will carry you safely to our Lord and you shall look upon His face."

Babushka's eyes fell upon her broom. Suddenly for the space of a single sentence she found the use of her tongue.

"Oh no, sir, thank you, sir, I cannot leave my house, sir. Why it taks me all day long to brush and sweep it."

The Third looked upon her with pity in his eyes; the First gave the signal. The procession moved on silently through the snow. Babushka stood and watched until its last shining jewel had passed from sight.

The next morning, when she awoke, it seemed to her all a dream. Surely the great Kings had not come; surely she had not refused to follow them. As swiftly as could be, she jumped from her bed.

A bit of ash had fallen on the hearth. Babushka looked for her broom. No, it was not in the corner; no, it was not in the cupboard; no, it had not fallen behind the stove. Where was her broom? Then she remembered. Her broom, why she was sweeping the sill with it when the Three, when the dream came. She opened the door. There almost buried was her broom. All through the night the snow had been falling; all the footprints and the tracks of the carts had been hidden, but there was her broom.

Babushka stepped inside. How sweet her little house smelled. What could it be? Why, it was Babushka herself. The Ethiopian King had dropped a bit of his precious myrrh upon her sleeve. The tears filled Babushka's eyes. It had not been a dream. She *had* left her broom there. She still bore the marvelous fragrance. They had come and gone.

At that thought Babushka was filled with a kind of madness. They had gone to see the King. She would hurry, she would find them, she would catch up with them. All her life she would search until she looked into the face of the King. Babushka threw down her broom, wrapped her cape about her, and without waiting for her boots ran out the door.

The days passed, and the years. Babushka hunted and searched. Her dark hair became gray, then white. Her little house was half filled with snow. She was as likely to run out leaving her door open as to close it. The paint was dull, the furniture marred, mats of cobweb lay in the corners, the hearth was strewn with ashes. Babushka was searching, searching, searching. . . .

One day she met a man who told her that after thirteen days the Three Men of the Orient had reached their goal and departed again. They had found the King. He was a Child born in a stable, wrapped in swaddling clothes and lying in a manger.

When Babushka heard that the King was a Child, her heart swelled and nearly broke with longing. "I must find him, I must hunt," she said. On and on she rushed, mile after mile. Wherever she saw a child, she looked long into his face. All her savings she spent for toys and sweets.

Sometimes a nurse or mother would come at night into the nursery, hearing the baby of the house crow and gurgle. There bending above him they would catch a glimpse of a strange old figure with young eyes. Like a breath of wind, she would be gone. In the morning, a bright carved chicken or a tiny duck would be lying in the child's crib.

"Ah," the nurse or mother would say, "Babushka has been here."

"Ah," all the children would cry, "Babushka was in this very room last night."

One day Babushka met a traveler who told her that the King had grown to be a man long ago, and that long ago he had died upon the tree. When she heard this, Babushka cried out with pain. The Child was a Man; the Child no longer lived; she would *never* find Him. But soon she half forgot this. More and more clearly she remembered the long gleaming procession of the Three Men, more and more she longed for the Child whom she sought.

In the house, out of the house, up the road, down the street, in castle, in hotel, in farmhouse, in hostelry, in stable went the old woman, swift and silent. When the children saw her they wrinkled up their noses. Something smelled so sweet! The toys she gave them they liked best of all; they kept them for their children and their children's children.

On and on, forever and forever, Babushka searches. A sound on the stairs, a laugh from the babe, a gift on the hearth. "Ah," sing the children, in joy, "Babushka is hunting for the King, hunting, hunting. But see the toys she left us."

In every home in Russia at Christmas time, when there are pretty gifts for boys and girls it is Babushka who is the giver. Babushka, who is searching, searching, searching.

The star of Bethlehem still shines, beckoning us to follow until we have found the Christ. And when we find Him and kneel before His altar, our lives will be changed. Grievous though our sins may have been, though the best years of our life have been devoted to serving the world and the devil, we cannot find Him and not "depart by another way"—the way of purity, of life and of truth—

the way which brings peace that passeth all understanding—the way of the cross.

May we also with shepherds and wise men, "Come and worship Christ the new-born King." And may we depart by that lighter and nobler way which leads at last to that bright home above.

Jesus stands at the door and knocks. And will you keep him waiting there?

Phillis Wheatley Home
Christmas Annual, 1922

A Merry Christmas to all our readers and all our friends. This day they are nearly all situated in the bossom of their families. Let them give thanks for the return of another Christmas Day and believe that they all have our best wishes for a Merry Christmas.

Bloomington Daily Pantagraph, December 25, 1865

ACKNOWLEDGEMENTS

Special thanks to the Illinois State Historical Society, Springfield; the Chicago Historical Society; the Galena-Jo Davies County Historical Society; the Newberry Library; and the public libraries of Rockford, Peoria, Chicago, Bloomington, Galena, Freeport and Ottawa.

"Christmas in the Lincoln White House" from *Tad Lincoln's Father* by Julia Taft Bayne.

Irish-American Folk Song from Mr. Dooley's Chicago "the Immigrant Experience."

"A Swedish Celebration" by Gloria Jahoda from the *Chicago Tribune*, December 4, 1960.

"The Christmas Tree Ship" from the book *The Chicago* by Harry Hansen. Farrar, Strauss, 1942.

"It's Good to Be Black" from book of same title by Ruby Berkley Goodwin.
Doubleday Publishing, a Division of the Bantam Publishing Group, Inc., used with permission.